JIMMY COATES: ASSASSIN?

JIMMY COATES: ASSASSIN?

JOE CRAIG

HarperCollins*Publishers*

To Mary-Ann Ochota, *sine qua non*

Jimmy Coates: Assassin?

Copyright © 2005 by Joe Craig

Library of Congress Cataloging-in-Publication Data

Craig, Joe, date.

Jimmy Coates: assassin? / by Joe Craig. — 1st ed.

p.   cm.

Summary: While escaping from the strange men that are after him in London, Jimmy discovers he possesses many unusual talents for an eleven-year-old boy.

ISBN 0-06-077263-8 — ISBN 0-06-077264-6 (lib. bdg.)

[1. Robots—Fiction. 2. London (England)—Fiction. 3. England—Fiction. 4. Adventure and adventurers—Fiction.] I. Title.

PZ7.C84419Ji 2005   2004025963

[Fic]—dc22

Typography by Christopher Stengel

2 3 4 5 6 7 8 9 10

❖

First American Edition, 2005

Originally published in Great Britain in 2005 by HarperCollins*Publishers* Ltd.

Thank you to the whole HarperCollins team, particularly Melanie Donovan, Stella Paskins, and Mark McVeigh. Thank you to Ann Tobias, Sarah Manson, and my family.

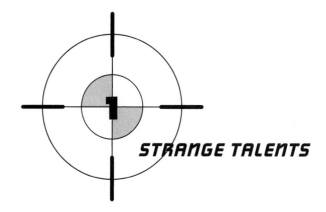

STRANGE TALENTS

Jimmy took aim, made sure his mother wasn't watching, and flicked. The chocolate wrapper hit his father, who grinned and returned fire.

"Stop messing about and help clear the table," Jimmy's mother said, chuckling and taking two plates to the kitchen. She ruffled her husband's hair as she passed him.

"Jimmy, I need your computer." It was Georgie, Jimmy's older sister.

"No way," he replied.

Georgie waited until both their parents were in the kitchen.

"I wasn't asking," she whispered. "Anyway, you can't stop me—I'm still bigger than you."

"Mum!" Jimmy cried.

"I'm not doing anything!" Georgie shouted in response. Their father popped his head round the door, back to being a grown-up.

"Keep it down. You'll disturb Mr. Higgins."

Too late—they heard the familiar pounding on the wall.

"I hate that old weirdo," muttered Georgie. It was remarkable how a next-door neighbor who claimed to be nearly deaf could have such sensitive hearing.

Jimmy slowly stacked the dishes.

"Come on, Jimmy," his sister pleaded, "I need to do that stupid project on Westminster Bridge."

"Okay." He sighed. "Half an hour. But if you want to find out about a place you should go there, not read about it on the Internet."

"Thanks for the advice, genius." Georgie ran up the stairs.

Once the table was clear, Jimmy joined his parents in the living room. They were watching the news. On the screen were pictures of Ares Hollingdale, the prime minister, walking around Downing Street, and then another man who looked a bit scruffier but a lot younger.

Jimmy wasn't interested in the news, so he turned to go, but his father's voice stopped him.

"Sit down, Jimmy—this will make a change from the rubbish you always watch."

"It's boring," replied Jimmy.

"But it's important—someone might form an opposition to the government again." He frowned for a second at Jimmy's mother, who pursed her lips.

Just then, the doorbell rang.

Jimmy's father pushed himself up with a sigh.

"You expecting someone?" asked his wife.

He stood for a long time scratching his ear, then just said, "No," and strode out to the front door.

Jimmy's father manufactured bottle tops for various soft

drinks and beers. He often saw clients at home, but these meetings always took a long time and sometimes went on late into the night. Sometimes Jimmy heard shouting when he was in bed.

"You don't think—," started Jimmy's mother, but her husband had already left the room. She looked at Jimmy. "Go upstairs and get ready for bed," she snapped.

"What?" said Jimmy. "Dad was just telling me to watch the news. And Georgie's in my room." His mother didn't answer. She turned off the television, and they both started listening to what was going on at the front door.

"Oh, it's you," Jimmy's father said. "I didn't expect—"

"Can we come in, Ian?" It was a man's voice, deep and flat.

"Erm, of course. We weren't expecting you." His father sounded nervous, and the other man cut him off.

"Thanks," he said. The floorboards creaked and the door opened. The man who walked in was tall and broad, taller even than Jimmy's father, and obviously in much better shape. He was tanned, and good-looking, but only smiling with one half of his mouth, a small smile that scanned the room and found Jimmy.

"Hello, young man. You must be James." Before Jimmy could answer, his mother jumped up between them.

"Please," she said, with her hand out to distract the man's attention. "Sit down. Please sit down."

The man looked at Jimmy's mother and straightened his tie. It was a long black tie, thinner than the ones Jimmy's father wore for work, and the man's suit was the same black.

"Helen, how lovely to see you again," he said, and sat where Jimmy's father had been sitting.

"Jimmy, go upstairs," said his father, who walked in and sat down awkwardly.

"No, he can stay, Ian," said the man in the suit.

"You haven't—," started Jimmy's mother, but the man cut her off.

"We've come for the boy."

There was silence.

Jimmy replayed in his mind what the man had just said: "We've come for the boy." What? Did that mean him, Jimmy Coates? Jimmy quickly went through the last few days in his head, or as much as he could manage on the spot, trying to remember if he had done anything wrong. But he was panicking and couldn't even think of what he'd done that morning, let alone yesterday or the day before. Then Jimmy suddenly noticed another man, who was standing in the doorway. He was dressed the same way as the first man, but was not quite as tall or as tanned.

Jimmy's father turned from one man to the other.

"You're early," he said. "We thought—"

"I know," the man interrupted again. "This is the new arrangement. We've come to get him." The man looked straight ahead, not around at Jimmy, and not at either of his parents. He was waiting for something. Finally Jimmy's mother spoke—and she surprised everyone.

"Run, Jimmy," she said, gasping, her voice almost a whisper. She clutched at her throat, and then shouted, "JIMMY, RUN!"

For a tiny moment he didn't move. Everyone's face was turned toward him. Jimmy looked at his father. He looked sad, but not scared like Jimmy's mother. The terror in her voice made its way into Jimmy's belly and connected with the confusion in his head. Then he was finally able to unfreeze his legs and throw himself toward the door.

The man standing there wasn't expecting such a burst of speed, and when Jimmy's full weight hit him, he was winded. Jimmy pulled open the front door. But what if there were other men in suits waiting for him outside? Leaving the front door open, Jimmy bolted to the stairs instead, sprinting up two at a time. He reached the top out of breath, and dashed into his bedroom.

"That was no way half an hour," Georgie grumbled from the computer. Jimmy didn't answer. "Who was at the door?" Jimmy could hardly hear her for all the blood rushing through his head. Then the regular beat of a big man pounding up the stairs hit him in the heart.

"Call the police." Jimmy panted, diving under the bed.

"What?" Georgie gasped. Jimmy heard the door open and saw two sets of shiny black shoes pointing straight at him, like four vultures.

"Hey, who are you?" Georgie yelled. "Get out!"

"Take her downstairs," ordered one of the men.

"Police! Help!" Georgie's screams faded as she was carried away.

Then a face appeared next to Jimmy's, leering down under the bed. It was the taller of the two men. His huge hand grabbed Jimmy's shoulder and dragged him out. Jimmy stood rubbing his neck as the shorter man returned. There was no noise from downstairs. Why was everyone so quiet?

"Why do you want me?" he asked.

"Why are you running?" countered the taller man immediately.

"I don't know who you are," said Jimmy.

"You don't know who you are."

At first, Jimmy thought it was a slip of the tongue. Then he wasn't so sure.

"I'm Jimmy Coates. My name is Jimmy Coates, and I'm just a kid."

"Okay, Jimmy, I need you to come with us. You can trust me."

There is something very untrustworthy about a man who says "Trust me." This man's eyes were the color of steel, and from the way his shirt pulled across his chest, it looked like he was built of the stuff too. Jimmy stared back as hard as he could and tried to look tough, but this wasn't a game. Jimmy's throat tightened, and something behind his stomach stopped him from breathing properly. It looked like he had no choice but to go with these men.

Maybe Jimmy hesitated just a little too long. The taller man dipped his hand into his jacket, and Jimmy caught a glimpse of a pale leather holster. When the man's hand emerged, it was holding a gun.

"I just need you to come with us," he stated coldly, but Jimmy couldn't take his eyes off the gun. It was the first one he had ever seen, and it was pointed straight at him.

All of a sudden, the feeling of utter fear behind his stomach turned into something else. Jimmy felt a surge of energy, as if some powerful piece of machinery had been turned on. It quickly spread through his whole body. It was something he had never felt before, and he didn't know whether he liked it. In another moment, it bolted up the right side of Jimmy's neck and wrapped itself around his head. At that moment he stopped thinking. His mind cleared, and the feeling inside started acting for him. He dipped his body to one side and sprang forward. He was out of the line of fire now, and before the man could adjust, Jimmy put one hand on the gun and the other on the man's wrist. With a firm twist, he pushed the barrel up toward the ceiling and leaned down on the man's hand. There was a loud crack. The gun dropped to the floor, and the man clasped his trigger finger in pain.

Jimmy had moved so fast that the shorter man hadn't had time to react, but now he leaped forward. Jimmy darted away from his desperate grasp, then kicked the gun under the bed. He looked toward the door, but both men stood in his way; even though one was hurt, he was still ready to act. His half smile had turned into a grimace.

Jimmy was acting automatically—by instinct, not by thought. It was like watching someone in a movie. He saw the men move and could predict exactly where they were going to go by the way their weight shifted across the floorboards. As they lumbered toward him, Jimmy took a light step to the side and leaped backward.

He coiled his body into a ball and shut his eyes tight. The two men were stunned as Jimmy smashed through the window. Glass shattered everywhere, and Jimmy felt it falling with him. The air was suddenly cold. He screwed his eyes shut harder and waited to hit the ground.

As he fell like a lump of stone, Jimmy's brain crept back on. He had enough time for one thought to go through his head— why had he jumped out of the window? There was a paved drive below, and now he was probably going to die, or at least break every bone in his body.

Then he hit the concrete.

2

GREEN STRIPE

Jimmy didn't move. He had landed on his shoulder, and his eyes were still shut. Glass rained around and on top of him. He could hear it falling on the roof of the car that was parked next to him, and he felt some hitting the side of his face. He lay there, waiting for the pain. Why hadn't he blacked out? Then he thought maybe he *had* blacked out. Maybe he was in the hospital, and the whole misunderstanding about the men coming to get him had been cleared up.

But Jimmy knew that wasn't true. He brushed fragments of glass away from his eyes and opened them. He could see the light of a streetlamp winking at him. He didn't understand why there was no pain at all. He wiggled different parts of his body. Everything moved just as he wanted.

He rolled his neck as one last test to make sure he wasn't actually dead. He looked up to the sky, then saw his house and the broken window. Dad's going to kill me, he thought. For a second he thought he saw Mr. Higgins's bony nose, peeking through next door's curtains, but Jimmy's eyes were still bleary. Then he picked out two faces looking down at him out of the glass-lined hole. Those two really *will* kill me, he thought. But he didn't get a chance to panic. That strange feeling crept up on him again, like a tropical wave filling his insides. It moved faster this time and swooped up the side of his head. Jimmy tried to keep his mind switched on; he didn't like surrendering control of his body to whatever this was. It may have saved his life, but next time it tried anything as stupid as throwing him out of a window, the result might not be the same.

He couldn't stop it though. Now that he knew he hadn't been hurt by the fall, Jimmy wanted to spring up and run as fast as he could. But he didn't move. His body stayed exactly where it was until the two heads moved from the window. They were coming down for him. Run now, please, he thought, but still he didn't get up from the drive. Instead he tucked his elbows into his chest and rolled over twice until he was under the car. The ground was cold, and chips of glass stuck into him as he spun over them. He felt around the undercarriage of the car and found a place for his fingers to grip. Then, with just the strength of his forearms, he pulled his whole body off the concrete. He hooked his toes under a fold of metal and waited.

There was dust and grime all over him. He could feel grease crawling down his arms and dripping onto his face. Slowly, he paid attention to his thoughts again: If he had run, the men would have jumped into a car and chased him down. But what instinct had told him to stay put and to roll under the car when the men weren't looking? Then he noticed the ridiculous position he was in, clutching the underside of the car. Where had this strength come from?

Now the two men came running out of the open front door. Again, Jimmy could only see their shoes.

"No visual," shouted the shorter man, looking up and down the road.

"You were meant to stop him from getting out of the living room."

"He used his strength against me."

"That's rubbish. He doesn't know yet."

"Then how did he break your finger and jump out of the window?"

"Put it in the report."

Jimmy was getting more confused by the second. What didn't he know yet? Then he heard the crackle of a walkie-talkie.

"The boy's out. Establish a per . We have no visual," one of the men said. Jimmy saw th of feet run over to the back of a van that was parked eet outside the house.

"What are you doing?"

"You don't expect me to s n out, do you?"

"The dogs won't do any ou fool," was the response, but the van was already o mmy heard barking and saw two sets of paws padding around the driveway. Then the dogs dipped their noses to the ground, and Jimmy saw their faces, their mouths drooling in the lamplight.

"I brought down a sock," said one of the men. Then he pulled both the dogs toward him on the long leashes. "There you go, boy. Good boy. Go fetch."

The animals circled the car, creeping like thieves, every now and again lifting their faces for a second, then snorting back to the ground. Jimmy watched one of them getting closer, walking right along the side of the car. It stopped at the level of Jimmy's face, and sniffed around. He had read that dogs could pick up a scent better when it was wet, and the ground was definitely damp. Jimmy held his breath.

"Get those dogs back in the van. They'll only cut their paws on the glass."

Both dogs were pulled quickly away. Jimmy was relieved for the moment, but even more confused. Why hadn't they picked up his scent? Jimmy sniffed, trying to recognize his own smell, then realized that was silly.

Then came more footsteps and a voice Jimmy knew. "Are the handcuffs really necessary?" It was Jimmy's father coming out of the house.

"I'm afraid they are, Ian," said one of the men. Jimmy held on tight to the car, his knuckles going white. He watched the feet of his family marching out to the street. First he watched his father's, then saw that his mother had been allowed to put on some shoes instead of the slippers she had been wearing. Then came Georgie. She had also changed out of slippers and into sneakers. But then there was one more pair of shoes. There must have been another suit that he hadn't seen, who came in after Jimmy ran upstairs.

These shoes were an anonymous black, and shiny just like the shoes of the other two men, but something about them made Jimmy look twice. There was a pattern on the toe that he recognized from somewhere; he just couldn't work out where. He watched the slowly away from the house. He was sure he had seen those before then again, maybe the fall had given him strange ideas instead of bruises and broken bones.

Jimmy watched everyone stepping through the puddles.

One of the pieces of glass on the ground offered him a strange, distorted reflection of the people walking about. Everything was upside down, and he couldn't make out their faces, but he could see their outlines. He wondered if any minute somebody could catch a glimpse of him reflected in the same glass, or even see his whole face if there was a puddle that caught the light. Then Georgie unknowingly provided the perfect distraction. She picked up her foot and kicked out at one of the men, nearly hitting him.

"You're not taking me," she shouted. Jimmy felt a jolt of excitement. "Help! Police!" If anybody could fight, Georgie could, he thought, remembering all the times he'd been pinned on the bed with his head under her arm. He willed her to keep screaming; surely someone would hear and get help, but then his father's voice cut in.

"It's okay, Georgie; we don't want to cause trouble. Quiet now."

"No, I'm not letting them take me!" She was shouting louder, and then she kicked out again, this time landing a sharp blow in the middle of the man's shin.

"Hey," said the man, grabbing his leg and rubbing.

"I'm not going with you!" And she ran. Jimmy watched her feet disappear from view and thought he could hear her shouting something. It sounded like, "I'm going to help Jimmy."

They had a chance now. Maybe someone had heard Georgie shouting and would call the police. Maybe even Mr. Higgins would decide not to be so deaf just when it was important, and get them some help.

"Let her go. We don't need her," said the man who had been kicked.

"Your leg okay?"

"Stupid kid. You take these two in the van; I'll follow in the car."

"And how's your finger?"

"Shut up and put them in the van. The boy won't get far."

Jimmy wondered why they didn't seem to want Georgie. And why were they taking his parents? This was clearly no ordinary kidnapping. One suspicion had taken hold and wouldn't let go: that something about him made him the target of men in suits with guns, and that this something was connected to his sudden ability to jump out of windows without getting hurt.

Two engines started up. He had to get a look at the van. It was his only way of finding out who was taking his parents away.

He eased himself onto the ground and rolled out, just in time to see the back of a car pulling away. There was no license plate. It was a long black car with blacked-out windows. A large black van was in front of it. They prowled like cats, agonizingly slow.

As they turned at the bottom of the street, he saw the driver of the van in silhouette, with one front-seat passenger. That must be the third man, he thought, the one I didn't meet. The light of the streetlamps glinted off the windows, and something caught Jimmy's eye. It was the only thing about the vehicles that wasn't completely black. On the side of the van, toward the back, was a fine, vertical green stripe. It was just thick enough for Jimmy to make out and no more than ten centimeters long. In the same place on the car was an identical green stripe. He saw it for just a snatch of time, so short that as soon as he had seen it he doubted himself. The van and the car turned the corner, disappearing as if they had never been there.

Jimmy walked back to his house and for the first time noticed that he wasn't wearing any shoes. He picked his way through the broken glass, which wasn't easy in the dark. The front door was locked. Of course it was. They all thought Jimmy was on the run somewhere, loose in the suburbs of London.

Everything seemed very quiet. There was no traffic, just the low hum of the city and the sound of lonely cars somewhere in the distance. One of them had Jimmy's parents in it. Then he thought about Georgie. Where had she run off to? Did she think she was going to be able to find him? Jimmy shivered and wondered whether his sister was as cold as he was. At least she had shoes on.

He hauled himself up the wall at the side of the house and stretched over the gate to lift the latch. It swung open with a creak. He took another glance over his shoulder at the street, but couldn't see anything. Then he turned to the path that ran down the side of the house. It was darker than he had ever seen it.

Jimmy told himself not to be so scared. It was his own house, and he knew there was nobody there. Any noise, he told himself, was just a stray cat. He started repeating it in a whisper. "Any noise, it's just a cat."

As he made his way round to the back of the house, he started singing it quietly to the brightest tune he could think up. Barefoot, and singing about cats, Jimmy felt like an incompetent burglar. Car grease blackened his cheeks. When he caught his reflection in a side window, he thought it was almost funny.

Knowing it would be locked, he tried the back door. Then he looked for an open window, but there wasn't one. He considered climbing the front of the house to get back into his bedroom, but it would have left him too visible from the street.

Instead he picked up a rock from his mother's rock garden and slammed it through the kitchen window.

As much as there is any right way to break a window, Jimmy did it the wrong way. Afterward he remembered that people in TV shows always used their elbows, and put a blanket or something in the way. Jimmy had just pushed his hand straight through. Now there was more glass all over his clothes and falling onto his feet. Some had hit him in the face. Fortunately none went into his eyes. What had happened to his ability to do things right? If he did have some strange power to escape dangerous situations, it would be much better if it didn't just disappear when he needed it.

Jimmy reached in, undid the latch, and opened the window. When he had scrambled inside, the first thing he did was pick up the phone. There was no dial tone. All he could hear was the blood surging through his head and his short breaths. He found his father's cell phone, but the case was smashed. Jimmy quickly realized too that there wasn't any power in the house. He wasn't planning on staying anyway. He couldn't just wait at home while his sister was in the streets on her own and his parents were being taken away in a van.

Jimmy tried to think quickly of all the things he might possibly need, but his heart wouldn't slow down enough to let him. What's more, he didn't even know where he was going or who he was running away from. He went upstairs for his schoolbag and threw the books onto the floor, replacing them with a change of clothes and an extra sweater. Then he picked out some food from the fridge: as much as would fit in the bag. There were some chocolate bars as well, and he grabbed an apple, in case he really got desperate. He opened the freezer and reached around at the back until he found the wad of cash that his mother kept there for emergencies and pizza. Finally he jammed his feet into some shoes, still wearing his wet socks with glass trapped in the fibers.

As a last-minute thought, he went looking for a flashlight. He knew there was one in the house somewhere. He ended up on all fours searching in the bottom of a kitchen cupboard. It was then that he caught sight of his wrist. There was a huge piece of glass sticking out from the base of his left hand. But it didn't hurt. He hadn't even noticed it until now: a lethal shard of glass.

He carefully pulled it out. It had gone deep into his flesh, more than a centimeter, but there was no blood. Jimmy wiggled his fingers. He clenched his fist. It seemed fine. There was a cut in his skin where the glass had been, but instead of being red, there was just a deeper layer of skin that looked sort of grayish. That had never been there before. He should have been bleeding to death by now. He considered putting a bandage over the cut, and even prodded it a few times, but decided that as it didn't hurt, it would be a waste of time to administer first aid in the dark. He spotted the flashlight and calmly popped it into the top of his bag, then went to sit at the kitchen table.

The house was completely quiet. Jimmy had never realized how lonely silence could be. He stared at the door and couldn't help imagining his parents walking in, all smiles and jokes. Two mugs waited by the kettle for someone to pour tea. But nobody was coming back. He had never felt so alone.

It was all so strange, he thought, but the strangest thing of all was him. He went up to his bedroom and looked down at the fall he had made.

The glass shimmered like broken stars, and a black tear

dripped down Jimmy's cheek. He wiped his face, smudging grease onto the back of his sleeve, then looked again at his wrist. What was this inside him? What had made him jump out of the window? He thought about why he hadn't been hurt in the fall, and why he wasn't bleeding now. A second later he heard his mother's terror in his head. Why had his father let those men into the house? Why had his parents walked away with them so calmly, and why had Jimmy's father not wanted Georgie to shout for help?

Jimmy picked up his bag, ran downstairs, and out of the front door. If he was going to help his family, he would have to get away from the house and not come back. And he needed the police. When the men in suits came looking for him, there would be more of them. Maybe he should learn to fight like he had in his bedroom, whenever he wanted. Otherwise he was just an eleven-year-old boy with a dirty face.

Jimmy started walking in the direction the van had gone. The suburbs of London swallowed him up; one semidetached family house after another in a groaning mess. Thousands of people were asleep in their beds, and Jimmy walked past their front doors trying to remember where the police station was. After a time he walked almost without direction. The street-lights just seemed to make the shadows darker, so that was where he walked, wary of anything that looked like a black car with a green stripe.

He let out a yawn the size of the city and didn't notice the thin, dark figure of the only other person in the shadows that night.

It had started following him.

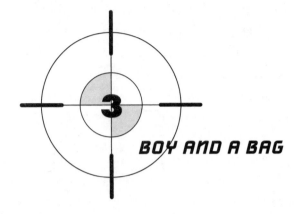

3

BOY AND A BAG

Mitchell had had quite a day. Twice he'd nearly been caught lifting a wallet from someone's bag, and both times he had been forced to drop whatever he had his hands on and run. So yesterday he had come out into a part of the suburbs he knew, to work the commuters as they left the subway stations. But they were always in such thick bunches that it was hard to get among them without arousing suspicion.

Now the streets were really quiet, and he was beginning to abandon hope of stealing anything for the day. He thought about the smell in his brother's apartment and didn't feel the urge to rush back there. Besides, he knew how hilarious his brother would find it if he came home empty-handed again. Mitchell didn't like being a thief, and he didn't much like his brother either. He especially didn't like living with him, but it was the only place he could go until he was old enough to get his own place. And his brother only let him stay on the condition that Mitchell would steal for him.

At first he'd been good at it—beginner's luck maybe. He was certainly fast when he needed to get away, and being a kid had its advantages; it meant he stood with his head at about the height of most people's shoulder bags. The last few days, though, had been really tough. He was tired and miserable. He didn't want to go home, but there wasn't much point roaming the empty streets and getting cold.

Then Mitchell heard the soft squeak of someone's sneakers behind him and turned to look. In the dim light he made out a single hunched-up shadow with a bag over its shoulder. Looks like a kid, he thought. He started to move closer, but realized that this person was shuffling straight toward him. Mitchell jumped over the low wall of a front garden and ducked down. Just a few seconds later, he watched a young boy with black grease all over his face walk past, not even a meter away. Mitchell could easily have reached out and tripped him up, grabbed the boy's bag, and run off. That's what his brother would have done, but there was too much risk that he'd wake up the people in the houses. Mitchell was smart—a lot smarter than his brother. He decided to be patient. He so badly wanted to end the day with a big catch. He couldn't mess this up. He would wait until this easy target was somewhere a little more open. Maybe this kid will be stupid enough to cut through the park, he thought.

Softly skipping back over the wall, Mitchell crept along the streets, keeping step with his prey.

Jimmy knew he had to get to the police station quickly. If those men were still looking for him, being out on the street was too dangerous. But every time he thought he had remembered the way, he turned a corner and everything became unfamiliar. It was eerily quiet, which made his steps seem horribly loud.

He wondered whether to knock on someone's door, waking someone up to ask for directions, but all the houses looked so sinister. Outside one, he even thought he saw a green stripe on the gatepost. He looked again, but it was just a brass number one that had rusted. It can't be far, he thought. I'll recognize one of these streets soon. But all the streets were mixed up in Jimmy's head, and he was really tired now. Each time he tried to pick his feet up, they felt like they had been stapled to the pavement.

"Pull yourself together," he whispered, and stopped outside the next house. He looked it up and down, then took a step through the front gate.

Just as he did, a flash of movement at the end of the street caught the corner of his eye. Jimmy turned his head ever so slightly. Was it a glint of light bouncing off a car window—or did it come from inside the car? He told himself it didn't matter—that tiredness and shock were making him paranoid.

Jimmy stepped slowly back through the gate and into the street. He squinted at the car. He could see something reflected in its side mirror: the faint orange dot of the end of a cigarette, muted by its own smoke. In the dark it shone out like a torch. This doesn't mean anything, Jimmy thought. It's just someone sitting in their car, smoking—I'm safe. But then the click of a car door opening jammed through his body. He froze. The cigarette light danced around rapidly. A man pulled himself up out of the car, and suddenly the silence splintered into a patter of noise: the car door slamming shut, the other door opening, the crackle of a walkie-talkie, two men walking toward Jimmy.

The driver flicked his cigarette into the gutter and picked up his pace. He was running straight at Jimmy, but Jimmy wasn't scared anymore. All the fear and tiredness drained out of his body, pushed away by that bundle of strength that grew from behind his stomach. It swept through his body and shot up his neck. Jimmy still didn't have any idea what was happening to him, but he recognized the feeling and knew this time that it was going to protect him. His feet leaped off the pavement and he broke into a sprint.

Jimmy's legs were possessed, carrying him and his bag as if they were no weight at all. His whole body was contorted into a running machine—arms pumping hard, head leaning intently forward. He had never moved so fast. He dashed up the street for a few meters before darting into a side alley between the houses.

For half an hour Mitchell had followed Jimmy, completely unnoticed. When Jimmy stopped, Mitchell stopped. As Jimmy stood in front of that house, wondering whether to knock on the door, Mitchell crouched in the shadows watching, wondering whether this was the moment to strike. Just as he decided to go for it, he saw two big men running at Jimmy from the other direction. Mitchell abruptly stood upright, shocked— his one chance to salvage the week was being ruined because two other guys had decided to mug the same person. He watched, bemused.

But then he saw that these two men were wearing suits and carrying walkie-talkies. Not even gangs dressed like that, or had such fancy equipment. The thought crossed Mitchell's mind that maybe this boy was in danger. Then Mitchell saw Jimmy explode into a run. Wow, he thought, that boy is quick.

The men seemed startled when Jimmy took off so smartly, and were slower to get going, but Mitchell could tell they were used to running. He waited until both men had made it to the top of the alley, then followed as fast as he could. If the men didn't catch this boy, then maybe he would.

Jimmy couldn't believe how fast he was running. His breathing was hard, but regular. Even with the bag over his shoulder he could feel his muscles moving together, blood surging through them. Something in his head was telling him where to run, too. It kept him darting in and out of back streets, knocking over garbage cans, leaping in and out of front gardens. A few moments ago he had been lost, exhausted and ready to give up, but now he was exhilarated. His feet tapped lightly on the paving stones, never stopping. Behind him there was the noise of heavier feet. Jimmy didn't look back. Still not out of breath, he began to enjoy the thrill of running, even though he felt like he wasn't in control.

The two men were slowing down now. Jimmy could hear them dropping back. He smiled and the wind cut into his teeth. At the next corner he found himself on a main road, and then he realized why the men had stopped running so hard. Two black cars zoomed toward him, headlights blasting him in the face. He hesitated for an instant, then ran again.

In a few seconds the cars were level with him. Jimmy ducked into a side street. The cars turned with him. He longed for his legs to do something more for him. Then they did—but it wasn't the extra burst of speed that Jimmy was hoping for. Instead, he hurdled over a front gate and down the side of a house. In two leaps he was up onto the wall and over the gate into someone's back garden. He took a hefty kick at the soccer ball lying on the lawn and saw that the back of the garden was surrounded by a high fence. It must have been twice as tall as he was. Behind him the garden gate was rattling.

Jimmy didn't stop. He couldn't. He sprinted forward and with three huge steps he left the ground. He reached up for the top of the fence and grabbed it with both hands. Then before he could process what was happening, he had pulled himself over. His knees buckled as he landed. He staggered for a couple of meters before regaining his balance, then looked around, wiping the sweat from his face with his sleeve. In front of him lay the dark oasis of the park.

Mitchell was still running. He saw the two men give up the chase, and he thought all the complications were over. Now he could catch the boy himself and take his bag. No problem. He zipped past the two men. They were bent double and completely out of breath. He hit the main road. It was only then that he realized how long he had been running, and how far.

He saw the two cars steaming after Jimmy. This boy doesn't have a chance now, Mitchell thought. He stood still for a second and watched Jimmy running away from the cars, amazed and a little impressed too. As soon as Jimmy turned, Mitchell started running again. The desire to steal Jimmy's bag was matched now by curiosity. He didn't feel tired and was hardly short of breath, but he stopped at the top of the road that Jimmy had turned down, astounded at what he saw.

The cars screeched up to the curb, and four men jumped silently out of each. All eight were in dark suits. Mitchell watched them burst through into the back garden, then return moments later. They didn't have the boy. One of the men started babbling into a walkie-talkie, his face red from running in the cold.

Mitchell was confused. How could they not have caught him? He hung back, so as not to be seen. Then Mitchell realized how the boy had managed to escape—the park was behind that row of houses. Once you were in the park at night, there were no lights. That's why it was one of Mitchell's favorite places to snatch bags.

He jogged back round the corner and headed for the entrance to the park. If he was quick enough, he might catch up with the boy as he ran out. It looked like the others had had the same idea, though, because they had climbed back into their cars and were heading that way themselves. They were driving slowly, though, as if they weren't sure where they were going, or even as if they wanted to give the boy a chance to get away.

Mitchell hunched his shoulders as they drove past, half from the cold and half out of an instinct not to be noticed. Then he realized they were looking at him. A flashlight shone right into his eyes. He flinched and put his hand up to block the beam. It lingered for a moment, then the cars moved stealthily on like a funeral procession. A streetlight caught a small green stripe at the back of each as it drove away.

Mitchell turned the corner and checked that the cars had gone. He was about to give up and go home, but he couldn't get the boy out of his head. There must be something in the bag really worth having.

The park gate was locked, of course, so he shinned up the

side and swung his body over. He had caught his jeans on the spikes at the top so many times now that it didn't bother him. On the other side he let himself drop into the dust, and brushed a twig from his hair. It needed the clippers again. Now his blood was pumping again, warming him up. He searched the park, picturing the riches he refused to miss out on.

Jimmy sprinted on for a minute, then slumped to the ground and held his breath. He listened, to find out whether the men had followed him over the fence, but they hadn't. Then all his tiredness hit him again. The ground was cold and wet, so he put his bag underneath him.

He knew the park, and while it was a relief to find a familiar place, it looked very different at night. He was afraid. It wasn't just two men who were after him. There were loads of them. In his memory, the sound of the group chasing him was magnified into a whole army. How could he possibly escape? In fact, how *had* he escaped? He had never run like that before.

Now that he had cooled down from the chase, he was shivering. Those men in the car had been waiting for him. But how had they known he was going to be walking down that particular street? Jimmy hadn't even known it himself. Then he had a sudden flash of being under the car in his driveway at home, and hearing the hiss of a walkie-talkie for the first time that night. "Set up a perimeter," one of them had said. There must have been men waiting for him in all the streets around where he lived. But why?

Jimmy stood up and pulled the extra sweater out of his bag. He took off his jacket and pulled the sweater over the one he was already wearing. Then he squeezed his jacket over the top and sat down on his bag, against a tree. He shoved his hands into his pockets, but couldn't bring himself to shut his eyes.

Instead he dug some food out of his bag and tried putting some of it together. His hands were too cold, though, and his attempt at a sandwich quickly fell apart. He munched on the debris. Then, suddenly, there was a shadow in front of him. The figure rested for a second with his hands on his knees, catching his breath.

"Give me your bag!" he hissed.

NEVER ALONE

Jimmy couldn't believe what he had just heard. He stood up and dropped the sad remains of his food. His mind was blank. He opened his mouth slightly, but nothing came out.

"Give me your bag," Mitchell repeated. Then shouted. "Did you hear me? Give me your bag!"

Jimmy looked down at his bag, dumbstruck. He had no idea what to do. He was even too surprised to be scared.

Mitchell was fed up. This wasn't the reaction he had expected. It was actually making him a little nervous that Jimmy seemed to be considering his demand, assessing whether it was worth giving up the bag. Mitchell pulled himself up to his full height, which wasn't a great deal taller than Jimmy. His eyes flicked between the boy and his bag. Should he ask one more time? What if the boy didn't speak English? There was only one way to sort this out, he thought.

Shaking his head in disbelief, he strode forward. Jimmy didn't move. So Mitchell stuck out the palm of his hand and pushed Jimmy out of the way. Jimmy lurched back and felt a pain in his chest where Mitchell had made contact. As Mitchell reached down for the bag, Jimmy came straight back.

At the split second that Mitchell bent over to pick up the bag, Jimmy jammed his foot into the back of Mitchell's knee and dug it in. Mitchell collapsed forward, then looked round, furious. Pulling the bag up with him, he swung it at Jimmy's head, but Jimmy was too fast. He ducked with ease and caught Mitchell's arm as it swung past, pulling it down and toward him. Mitchell didn't have the balance to stay upright and reeled forward. His face hit the ground this time, and it wasn't kind. Jimmy planted his foot firmly on the back of Mitchell's neck.

"Let go of the bag," he said. He sounded calm, but inside Jimmy was amazed at his own speed, strength, and reactions. He had watched himself moving and seen someone who really knew how to win a fight. There was no fuss, just efficient and devastating moves. The violence in him had sprung from nowhere, telling him what to do, or doing it for him.

Mitchell had never stood a chance. His face was squished against the cold dust. He couldn't feel anything except the pressure against his neck that was so close to cutting off his breathing. That and shame. The physical discomfort was matched by the pain of injured pride. He opened his fingers slowly, letting the strap of the bag fall.

Jimmy kicked it away but kept his eyes fixed on the back of Mitchell's head. In the dim light he could make out the glistening of a tear on Mitchell's eye as it rapidly blinked, trying to throw off the soil of the park. Then, with a rush of awareness, Jimmy felt terrified by what he had done. Until tonight it had been completely alien to him to act in such a violent way. Now he stood there, with power over another boy. He had it in him to do terrible things when hardly provoked. He could have given up his bag and then found his way to the police station. But he hadn't.

Jimmy's first instinct was to step back and apologize, to help the boy up off the ground, even. But there was nothing to stop the fight from continuing if Jimmy released his opponent now.

"Leh we go!" Mitchell cried from the ground, his words obscured by grass and fear.

"Okay," Jimmy said, thinking desperately, "but you have to help me."

"Whaa?"

"Help me."

"Jush gid your fuh off why nick!"

"What did you say?" Jimmy lifted his foot and stepped back. Mitchell rolled over to look up at him.

"I said, 'Get your foot off my neck.'"

"Oh." For the first time, Jimmy could look squarely into this other boy's face. Mitchell stood up carefully, not taking his eyes off Jimmy, and reluctantly rubbed his neck. Jimmy was surprised to see that the person who had tried to mug him was so young. "How old are you?"

"Sixteen," said Mitchell.

"You're not sixteen. You're shorter than my sister, and she's thirteen." Jimmy felt a new confidence. He didn't think this boy would be too keen to have a foot in his neck again.

"So? I might be short for my age."

"You're no way sixteen, that's all." Jimmy looked at him harder, as if to check.

"All right, I'm thirteen," mumbled Mitchell, his humiliation complete. He looked away.

"There's nothing in my bag," Jimmy remarked. "Just food and clothes."

"Then why were all those men after you?"

Jimmy tried to think of an answer, but nothing came. He knew it wasn't for the bag, though.

"They're after m-me," he stuttered, at last. The shock of hearing it said aloud for the first time was dreadful. "They're after *me*," he said again. His throat tightened, and his stomach turned over. This wasn't any mysterious inner strength, though—it was fear.

"What's your name?" said Mitchell.

"Jimmy."

"I'm Mitchell. Hi."

"I don't want to fight." Jimmy suddenly felt close to crying.

Mitchell let out a huge laugh, throwing his head back and feeling his neck some more. Jimmy was taken aback.

"What's funny?"

"You idiot. You just beat me up. You could have killed me," scoffed Mitchell. "I'm not going to try hitting you again, am I? Idiot."

"Shut up!" said Jimmy, but a small part of him glowed at this coming from an older boy. "Just go away."

"I'm not running away. What if you chase me?"

"I won't chase you."

"I'm staying here. If you want to go, then go. I'd never catch you." Mitchell stepped slightly to the side, almost inviting Jimmy to run past him. But something Mitchell had said made Jimmy stay.

"You saw them chasing me?" Jimmy asked.

"What? Yeah. I saw those men get out of the car and come at you."

"You watched the whole thing? And you could keep up?"

"Well, yeah. Sure." Mitchell shrugged his shoulders. "I dunno, I'm a fast runner too, I guess. Faster than those men, anyway."

"Oh." Jimmy wondered how come two kids had been able to run faster and farther than any of the men.

"So, are you going?" Mitchell jerked his head to one side, indicating the park.

"I need your help."

"Yeah right. What for?"

"I just need you to take me to the police station."

"What?" Mitchell laughed again, but it was more nervous this time. "You want me to go with you to the police station so you can tell them to arrest me? Do you think I'm stupid?"

"No, not so they can arrest you. You don't have to come in with me, but I need to get away from those men."

"Why should I help you? I already saved you from them."

"What?"

"I saved you from those men. They were going to catch you, but I stopped them."

"You didn't stop them. I escaped."

"Yeah, I did. You don't know. You couldn't see." Mitchell jumped from foot to foot, half from cold and half from rest-lessness. Jimmy knew he was lying. It was pretty obvious. He didn't want to argue, though. He wanted to get moving before the men found him again.

"Okay, whatever. Thanks." Jimmy sighed. "So because you

saved me, I won't tell them you tried to steal my bag. But you still have to take me to the police station. Unless you want my foot in your neck again." He had never threatened anyone like that before, and he didn't like how it felt, although he could see from Mitchell's expression that it was going to work.

"Why don't you phone them? Get out your cell phone." Mitchell thought he was being clever. His brother would be impressed if he snatched a cell phone.

"I don't have one. What about a phone booth?" said Jimmy, completely unaware that the truth had saved him from another attempt at robbery.

"Whatever. Come on, then. Let's go."

Mitchell and Jimmy walked through the park in awkward silence. Mitchell stayed a couple of steps ahead of Jimmy. He was used to walking alone and didn't like the feeling of accompanying someone. He dug his hands into his pockets and ignored the boy next to him.

Jimmy dragged along behind. It had been a very long night and it wasn't over yet. He longed to shut his eyes and find himself back in his bed, waking up from a bad dream. His parents would be there, so would Georgie, and everything would be fine—perhaps better than before. No arguments, and definitely no men in suits.

As they climbed through some bent railings in the park fence, Jimmy shot out a question just to break the silence. "What school do you go to?"

Mitchell grimaced. "Leave me alone."

"Oh." Jimmy waited a second, then tried again. "Hey, thanks."

"What?" This time Mitchell turned to look at Jimmy.

"Thanks for showing me the way. I was lost. What's your name again?"

"I can't believe I'm doing this." Mitchell sneered. "I should have beaten your head in."

"You didn't, though, did you?" Jimmy felt braver now. Compared to suited men in black cars, Mitchell was a lot less scary than he might have been. "I've forgotten your name," Jimmy said.

"It's Mitchell. But we're not friends, so you can forget it again."

"I'm Jimmy."

"I know. Jimmy the idiot."

Jimmy just smiled. Being called an idiot didn't seem to matter anymore. He didn't mind that Mitchell didn't want to talk; he was just relieved to have someone taking him in the right direction. And he might have been wrong, but he thought for a second that he saw a smile creep onto Mitchell's face.

They stopped on a corner.

"It's down there on the right," Mitchell muttered.

"Wait here," ordered Jimmy, straining to see if the police station was there. He kept Mitchell in the corner of his eye, just in case. "How do I know I can trust you?" he said at last.

"You don't." Mitchell shook his head in exasperation. "Look, it's down there, okay? I'm not taking you any closer. I'm not your mum. So believe me or don't; I don't care. I'm going home." He turned his back on Jimmy and started walking away. He was braced for a fight, expecting Jimmy to pounce on his back. He tried to walk casually.

All Jimmy could see were the shadows. He scoured the

scene for anything that looked suspicious. But everything looked suspicious. Any parked car could be concealing more men in suits, lying in wait for Jimmy. He didn't want Mitchell to leave. The company was comforting.

"Thanks again," Jimmy whispered.

Mitchell didn't look around. Instead he stuck his hand up in the air and held it there for a moment, then he broke into a jog and was gone. Jimmy's heart sank. He was alone again.

5

FACE OF A FOE

There it was. Hardly a hundred meters from where Jimmy had been hesitating, the police station sat like a comforting smile washed in blue light. It was set back from the road slightly, which was why he hadn't seen it from the corner. Now he ran through the door like it was home.

He rushed through the brightly lit lobby up to the desk. There was no one else in there except for the officer behind the desk, and another sitting on a bench by the door, nursing a bloody nose and holding an ice bag to his forehead. Jimmy threw a glance at him, but the officer looked away hurriedly and pretended to read the notice boards.

"Hello, son. Can I help you?" said the officer behind the desk. He spoke in a deep voice that sounded friendly to Jimmy, but at the same time a little scary. Maybe that was because it was coming from a man who was well over six feet tall. Jimmy had never actually spoken to a policeman before. His words tumbled over one another, confusing his tongue.

He didn't know where to begin.

"My parents . . . I was in my house . . . these men came . . . they chased me, but that was later . . . I don't know . . . and my sister, but . . ." Then Jimmy stopped because he realized he was crying. He let the tears come like warm comfort on his chilled face. The fluorescent lights blurred into his eyes, and the huge policeman came around to Jimmy's side of the desk.

"That's all right, Jimmy. Come and sit down." At the sound of his name, Jimmy immediately tensed up again and stopped crying. He felt the officer's huge hand on the top of his head. It guided him gently but firmly to the bench.

"I'm Sergeant Atkinson," said the policeman. He was limping, but trying not to show it. Jimmy had to step over a fire extinguisher that was lying on the floor and push past a small table. "That shouldn't be there; sorry," said the sergeant as he bent down. With one strong arm he snatched up the fire extinguisher, setting it upright next to the door.

The policeman with the blood all over his face stood up as soon as Jimmy sat down. He went past the desk and pushed through the doors, out of sight.

"How do you know my name?" Jimmy's voice was meek, quiet.

"Your neighbors called and told us everything that happened."

"Mr. Higgins?"

"No, Mr. and Mrs. Bourne."

Jimmy didn't know the neighbors on the other side. He had never even seen them. There was usually a car in the driveway, like there was in every driveway, but he had never seen anybody coming or going.

"Why didn't you go round to them for help when it all happened?" said Sergeant Atkinson.

"I don't know. I didn't think of it, I suppose." Jimmy considered whether he should have just gone next door, but it didn't feel right. It was too close to home. Surely by now his house was crawling with men in suits waiting for him to come back. They would have found him easily if he had just been next door.

"They would have helped you, Jimmy. They were waiting for you to come round."

"What do you mean, they were waiting? Why didn't they call the police? Call you, I mean?"

"They did, of course," explained the sergeant. "That's how we know what happened." Jimmy was starting to feel silly now, but he was sure he hadn't acted stupidly. It had all felt so dangerous—like he had to get away from the house as soon as he could.

"But . . . if they called the police," Jimmy stammered, "why didn't you come?"

"We did. But you had run off." Sergeant Atkinson patted Jimmy on the head as if to comfort him. But Jimmy was thinking. He was trying to push away the tiredness and the fear, forcing his thoughts and memories into some kind of order.

"But I didn't. I was at my house," Jimmy said, almost to himself.

The policeman stood up to welcome one of his colleagues coming through the swing doors behind the desk. It was a young policewoman, beaming at Jimmy.

"I was at my house," Jimmy said again.

Sergeant Atkinson turned around and gave him a questioning frown.

"No, you jumped out the window and ran off," he said.

"No, I— How did you know I jumped out the window?"

"The Bournes told us. They saw the whole thing. Your neighbors." The policewoman was speaking now. She was in uniform just like the others, but seemed a lot shinier. Maybe it was the smile. "There have been a lot of police officers looking for you all night," she said, in a way that made Jimmy feel like it was his fault.

"But, I was just—" Jimmy stopped himself. If so many people were looking for him, why hadn't he seen a single policeman? Or any police cars?

Jimmy stood up and wiped his face with the back of his sleeve.

"Who's after me? Why are they chasing me?" Jimmy was glad he'd had a chance to cry, to let out some of the confusion. Now his head was clearing. The lights in the station had woken him up a little too. He picked up his bag and shifted from foot to foot. The police officers looked at each other. It was the woman who spoke first.

"Don't think about that now. Let's get—"

"Who's after me? If you know, tell me." Jimmy had been through too much already to have secrets kept from him. But his question was only greeted with silence. "Why aren't you telling me?" Jimmy was getting more and more impatient, but it was hard to raise his voice at police officers. He waited a second, then he let go and shouted, "Why aren't you telling me?"

More policemen emerged at the back of the room. They were all big, and none of them was smiling.

"What are they all doing here if they're meant to be out

looking for me?" Something was wrong. It was obvious. There was no way that any neighbors could have seen him jump out of the window. And if anybody *had* been watching, they would have seen him hide under the car, then go back to the house.

The sergeant spoke at last, but it wasn't good enough for Jimmy.

"Sit down, Jimmy. You're tired and overexcited. We're here to help," he blathered.

"I'm leaving now," said Jimmy, edging toward the door. "Thanks for your help. I'll be okay, though." There were half a dozen policemen now. One of them strode over to the front door. One of them crossed his arms and stayed by the swing doors at the back. Another one slipped in behind the desk and put his hand on the receiver of the phone. Jimmy could feel that dark ball welling up inside him.

"I'm going to stay with my cousins, so I'll be fine." He tried to stop it, to push it back down, but it was fueled by anger now. Jimmy could feel it growing darker and larger than it had before. Please, he said to himself, don't try and fight all these policemen. Perhaps they're on my side. But in his heart, he was just uncertain enough.

"There's no need to go, Jimmy. We can sort this out."

"Good-bye." Jimmy leaped into the air, his sneakers squeaking on the linoleum, and dashed under the flailing arms of Sergeant Atkinson.

"Stop him!" someone shouted. The room erupted into chaos and hullabaloo. Jimmy felt himself moving, but couldn't influence his actions. Once again the animal instinct that had helped him survive that night had taken control of his limbs. He knocked over the table with his shin, but didn't feel any pain. Leaflets flew everywhere. Jimmy grabbed a notice board, shoving it in the way of a huge policeman as he dived. The policeman hit the floor, and Jimmy stepped on his back to springboard off it and slam his feet into Sergeant Atkinson's chest. Jimmy rolled under the desperate lunges of the other police, then bounded to his feet and rushed to the door. It was a big, heavy wooden door, but Jimmy crashed through it into the street. And ran.

The lobby of the police station was devastated. The policeman with the bloody nose reappeared through the swing doors and laughed, glad he wasn't the only one to have suffered that night.

Sergeant Atkinson picked himself up and dusted off his uniform. His huge jaw cracked as he ground his teeth. There was an impressed smile behind his eyes as he looked out through the door, broken off its hinges, into the early morning.

"Let him go; it's okay. We'll pick him up at his cousins'," he said. "Where do they live?"

The policewoman next to him looked down at her boots. Then she spat out the words: "He doesn't have any cousins."

Jimmy ran just like he had already that night, but this time he couldn't hear anybody following him. He ran longer than he needed to, just in case, until finally he started to feel weakness seeping into his knees. It was the strain that would normally have come ages ago. He slipped into a doorway and looked behind him. The street was empty. If anybody had been following him, they hadn't kept up.

Jimmy's legs twitched with fatigue. He bent over and rested

his hands on his knees, feeling the strength in him fade away. It didn't get any easier to understand. What was this strange urge in him to fight or to run? And how did he suddenly have the ability to do both? Jimmy wasn't sure he liked it. However wonderful this power was, the very fact of its presence was terrifying. Before tonight he'd been like every other normal boy.

What's more, he didn't like having a violent side. It wasn't just self-defense. Jimmy had been too keen to fight Mitchell, when he could have just handed over his bag and avoided anybody getting hurt. He imagined himself really injuring someone, or worse . . . but it made him wince and he shook his head hard.

Jimmy had to get off the streets. Everyone was after him. Everywhere was dangerous.

Jimmy caught sight of his fingers. They were purple with cold. He wished he had brought gloves. Even after he had been running so hard, sweating and red-faced, his fingers were bitten by the wind. Whatever happened, he didn't want to be stranded out on his own when the sun came up. The police would pick him up in no time. He hitched his bag higher on his back and started walking. This time he wasn't lost; from High Street he knew his way. Jimmy was heading to the place he considered his second home—the house of his best friend, Felix Muzbeke.

Jimmy trudged past the neatly trimmed hedges of the suburbs, consumed by his thoughts. He told himself over and over that he wasn't a criminal, but it did no good—he still felt like one. It was worse than that, though—this feeling was coupled with the indignation of innocence. He imagined himself back at the police station shouting into Sergeant Atkinson's leathery face: "I've done nothing wrong!"

Only one realization brought a smile to his face: He had busted out of the police station when at least six enormous officers had wanted to keep him there. First he had seen through their lies, then he had slipped through their fingers.

He shuffled toward Felix's road, munching on the last of his food: a chocolate bar and an apple. At the corner, he was shocked out of his reverie by a twitching curtain. And was that a green stripe on the gatepost? No—just a tired illusion. He kept his head down and walked on.

The Muzbekes' house was bigger than his, and a little smarter. Jimmy had no hesitation in ringing the bell, despite it being so early in the morning. When Felix's parents heard what had happened, they would have to understand.

He rang twice before he heard movement inside. There were faint voices, the clunk of two bolts, and then a look of utter bewilderment when Felix's father pulled open the door. His eyes were red and only open a tiny crack. He pulled his wife's flowery bathrobe round him with one hand to guard against the freezing cold.

Jimmy looked himself up and down as Neil Muzbeke did the same. He was a wreck: covered in grime, his shoes filthy from the park. He had torn his jacket too, probably going over a fence, or maybe in the fight at the police station, or . . . It could have happened anytime that night. No wonder it took the man a couple of seconds to recognize him. Felix's father shook his head and blinked.

"Jimmy?" he spluttered.

The house was warm, and washing the dirt off his face felt wonderful—not to mention the chance to sit down. Felix's parents were both up now, and his mother was fixing cups of tea. Felix himself hadn't stirred. Outside, the birds had started singing, and a gentle light was pushing through the windows. Jimmy sat at the kitchen table, unsure of what else to say. He had explained everything as calmly as he could, trying to be sensible and detached. At first, of course, they hadn't believed anything he said, but when they phoned Jimmy's house and there was no answer, they listened more closely.

"I'm going to call the police," fussed Olivia Muzbeke for about the tenth time.

"I told you, you can't. If you call the police, they'll come and take me away."

Felix's father cleared his throat and brushed his wild hair back from his face. "If you've done something wrong, Jimmy," he said, "it's okay to tell us, whatever it is. We won't be angry." His bulbous cheeks wobbled as he shook his head rapidly.

"I told you, I swear. I haven't done anything. They must be after me because of what I can do. I think maybe they want to experiment on me." Jimmy meant this sincerely, but when he heard the words come out of his mouth, he knew they wouldn't be taken seriously.

"Jimmy, dear," said Felix's mother, "if you have superpowers, you should show us."

"I can't show you. It just happened. I told you. It was this thing inside me that took over when I was in danger."

Mr. and Mrs. Muzbeke looked at each other. The ping of the electric teakettle broke the silence.

"You can sleep in the spare room." Felix's mother sighed. "I'll fetch you some of Felix's pajamas. We'll get this whole thing sorted out later in the morning."

Jimmy stood up from the table. He was exhausted. Later, when they found out his parents really were missing, they would have to believe him.

Then Jimmy remembered his sister.

"What about Georgie?" he said. "Call her school at nine o'clock, and I bet you she won't be there. I don't think they're after her too, but she ran off, and she's going to try and help me."

"Jimmy, go to bed," said Felix's mother. "Now."

Felix's father glanced up at the clock and groaned.

"I may as well get ready for work," he said. "What a start to the day."

Jimmy was upset. He knew he wasn't exaggerating, or imagining it all. He just had to prove it. He stopped at the door and turned around. Suddenly he started opening all the kitchen drawers.

"What are you doing?" shrieked Felix's mother. "Stop that. What are you looking for?"

It was too late. Jimmy had found a knife.

IN HIDING

Felix Muzbeke hated getting up in the morning. In fact, there was only one thing that he hated more: waking up five minutes before the alarm went off. Those five valuable minutes of sleep were lost to him forever, and not having those five minutes was going to make him tired all day. He knew trying to get back to sleep was pointless, so he thumped his hand down on the button that would stop the alarm from going off and trudged to the bathroom as if going to his execution.

It was when he reached the bathroom that he heard the noise from downstairs again and realized it must have been what woke him up. Felix looked across at his parents' bedroom door. It was ajar, which meant they were both up. He was ready to brush it off as a lively breakfast, but then he heard his mother shriek.

Felix knew that if there was something seriously wrong, he probably couldn't do anything to help, but nobody was ever more curious. A scream on a school morning was an unusual event. It would at least give him something to talk about at school. He trotted down the stairs and pushed open the kitchen door, then thought he must still be dreaming. "Oh my God! Hi, Jimmy."

His mother was sitting at the table with her face in her hands, quivering slightly. Felix's father was just staring back at him with his mouth half open and his eyebrows frowning. But it was Jimmy who had surprised Felix. First of all, he wasn't meant to be there. He also wasn't meant to have a huge kitchen knife sticking out of his arm.

"Hi, Felix," said Jimmy, happiness in his voice. He was genuinely delighted to see his friend. His left arm was stretched out on the kitchen table, his hand turned upward. At his wrist, the knife stood up on its own, with about a centimeter of the blade sunk into Jimmy's flesh. It rose like Excalibur and flashed in the gray morning light.

Felix's mother emerged from behind her hands. "Stop that at once! Put that thing down!" she squealed. But Jimmy just smiled, as calmly as he could.

"No, it's okay, look," he said. "It's like I was saying . . . ," and he curled the fingers of his right hand round the handle of the knife. Slowly he pulled the blade out of his wrist. "No blood. Told you."

Felix came right up close.

"That is so cool. Can I have a go?" Felix reached out for the knife, but his mother pulled him away.

"No! That is very dangerous and you shouldn't do it. Nor should you, Jimmy. Put the knife away." Jimmy didn't answer. He just held out his hand to Felix's father.

"Jimmy," said Mr. Muzbeke, "is this a trick?"

"No."

"And it did the same thing when you got glass in your wrist?"

"It was a big bit of glass from the window, and at first I didn't even notice it was there. It didn't hurt or anything."

Just like before, there was no blood, no mess, and Jimmy didn't feel any pain. Any normal person would be bleeding to death by now, but Jimmy just had a flap of skin. He could squeeze his little finger in and touch a deeper layer, which was slightly gray under the pink skin.

"What are you doing here, Jimmy? Are you coming to school with me?" Felix was a little disappointed about there not being an intruder or a major disaster for him to report on.

"Erm, I can't go to school, Felix, and you can't tell anybody I'm here."

"Can I tell them about your arm? Does it hurt?"

"No, you can't tell them, and no, it doesn't hurt."

"How come you look so terrible?"

While Felix bolted his breakfast, Jimmy tried as best he could to explain everything that had happened to him. Felix's parents kept interrupting, telling Felix to hurry up and telling Jimmy not to exaggerate. But even so, he began to feel that Mr. and Mrs. Muzbeke were starting to believe him. Felix was riveted.

"Okay, listen, I won't tell anybody you're here, but when I get home from school, we're going to check out your superpowers," said Felix. In a flash he was dressed and out of the door, sprinting up the road—very late.

"It doesn't feel like having superpowers," said Jimmy as the front door clicked shut. Felix's mother put her hand on the back of Jimmy's neck.

"Go and get some sleep. And don't worry about your family. I'm sure they're fine, wherever they are."

Jimmy dropped his head and yawned. He was so tired, he had stopped thinking straight a long time ago. He pictured the faces of his parents and his sister as he crawled up the stairs and into the unfamiliar bed. The spare room was too tidy, too clinical to be homely. It was obvious nobody stayed in there much.

The fact that it was light outside didn't matter. Jimmy closed his eyes and let his body curl into a ball. He didn't feel as excited about any of this as Felix obviously did. He certainly didn't feel like a superhero. He felt awful.

"He makes bottletops, for God's sake. Who could possibly want to kidnap Ian Coates?" Felix's mother was pacing the kitchen, trying hard to keep her voice down so as not to wake Jimmy.

"Jimmy thinks they're after *him*. Have you phoned the house again?"

"Still no answer. But that doesn't mean anything, does it?"

"I don't know." Felix's father rubbed his face with his hand, trying to banish the shock of a strange morning. He allowed himself a moment of self-pity. He worked so hard as it was, he didn't need to be woken up extra early by a runaway child. He put the kettle on again and shook his head. His dark jowls jiggled as if they had just woken up. "What should we do?" he asked finally.

"I'm phoning the police." Olivia Muzbeke walked over to the phone on the wall and picked up the receiver. Her husband was there in a flash.

"You can't do that," he said, and put his hand across the phone.

"Leave me alone; I'm calling the police. If Jimmy is telling the truth and something has happened to the Coateses, then the police need to know."

"If Jimmy is telling the truth, then the police are also trying to catch him."

Felix's mother knew her husband was right. She put down the phone.

"What if he's done something wrong?" she said as she poured yet more tea.

"You know him better than I do. Has he ever been in trouble before?"

"No."

"Has he ever done anything he shouldn't have?"

"He stuck my meat knife into his arm."

Mr. Muzbeke sighed. He looked up at the clock and thought about going to work. "We can let him stay for a couple of days. Until we know what's going on. But don't tell anybody he's here, and don't call the police. Not yet."

"That's so silly. It's all so ridiculous, Neil. . . ."

"Just in case. The state this country's in, I wouldn't be surprised if the police decided to abduct an innocent family. Would you?"

"Okay. A couple of days."

Jimmy slept a long time, but still didn't feel rested when he woke up. It had been happening quite a lot recently. He would wake up with the impression that he'd had a nightmare, but couldn't remember what it was. And he hardly ever felt properly rested. He opened his eyes and wondered what the time was. There was no clock in the room. All he could think about when he looked at the light coming through the curtains was that he'd jumped out of a similar window the night before. Suddenly he was filled with anxiety. What if the Muzbekes had told someone he was here? What if Felix had blabbed at school? He was a good friend, and he would never put Jimmy in danger deliberately, but he was always giving secrets away by accident.

An image jumped into Jimmy's mind that was too real for comfort. It was the picture of the Muzbekes' house surrounded by men in black suits, with their thin black ties oozing down their fronts. Then he pictured them in the kitchen, being served tea by Olivia Muzbeke, just waiting for Jimmy to come downstairs.

He shut his eyes and tried to go back to sleep, but all the tension from the night before had rushed back into his body. He slipped down below the duvet, wishing he could stay there forever, but quickly got too hot.

Downstairs, Felix was guzzling toast in front of the TV. There was toast waiting for Jimmy too. Felix's mother must have heard him getting up.

"Hiya, Jimmy, how's your arm?" Felix almost shouted this, and bounded over to punch Jimmy on the shoulder.

"Yeah, it's fine."

"Lemme see." Jimmy showed Felix his wrist and kept it held out while he sat down and started eating his toast. He let the images from the TV go into his brain without paying attention and felt Felix prodding around his cut.

"That's so cool."

"All right, get off it now." Jimmy pulled his arm back.

"Can I cut off your hand?" said Felix.

"What?" Jimmy glared at Felix, before he realized he was joking. Felix laughed, and after a second Jimmy did too. "How was school?"

"Okay, I suppose." Felix shrugged. "Miss Bennett nearly didn't even notice you were missing when she took attendance."

The more they chatted, the more ridiculous the events of the night before seemed. The danger started fading in Jimmy's mind; he didn't know why anybody was after him, so there didn't appear to be much point being afraid. But as the fear dwindled, in its place came a long, slow ache. The memory of his parents being driven away tore at his mind. Suddenly he knew what it meant to miss somebody.

"We should go and find them," Felix said brightly, with toast crumbs all over his face. "Your parents, I mean."

"What?"

"Well, you said we can't call the police, and they've disappeared, right? Taken by these strange men in suits." He said it like it was the name of an alien race, and waved his hands in front of him, trying to look spooky.

"It's not a game."

"Sounds like one to me. And it sounds like you're really good at it, too. I want to see you run."

"Well . . ."

"Could you throw me out the window?"

"Look . . ."

"Jump onto the ceiling and stick there. Go on."

"Shut up, would you? I can't just do stuff. I think it just

happens when I'm in danger."

"How do you even know you're in danger?" Felix was giving Jimmy one of his funny looks. "What if these people just want to take you to a holiday camp and feed you hamburgers for a week? What if they're an elite, hamburger-feeding force on the lookout for slightly chubby boys who have the right to be completely obese?" Felix puffed out his cheeks and started walking round the living room with his belly sticking out.

"I don't think they're trying to feed me burgers." Jimmy had to laugh. It was just what he needed. But he knew he was in danger. It was the darkness inside that told him. Jimmy tried to feel it in his stomach; there was only toast. He knew it was there, nonetheless. It was waiting.

They spent the rest of the afternoon in Felix's room, but were soon bored of computer games; since the ban on almost all American products, the new releases had been rubbish. The console kept breaking down, anyway. Instead, Jimmy had to describe over and over again how he had escaped all the different situations he had found himself in the night before. Felix kept jumping up to act them out—completely wrongly, of course. Jimmy was just glad that his friend believed him, and that the fun almost took his mind off his troubles.

"I bet you can fly," Felix said at last, when he had heard the story of the night from about six different angles.

Jimmy put a hand on his stomach, as if feeling for the answer. "No way," he muttered.

"How do you know if you haven't tried?"

Jimmy just shrugged. He was scared to think about what this thing inside him was capable of.

"You might have X-ray vision," Felix continued. "Or lasers

that come out of your fingers."

"Whatever."

Felix turned his back on Jimmy and sauntered over to the other side of his room. Suddenly, he clasped his fingers round his bedside lamp and flung it at his friend, ripping the plug out of the wall.

Jimmy was hardly more than a meter away, but instinctively he reached out and caught the lamp in one hand. The plug at the end of the wire came at his face, but he plucked it out of the air. Then he dove at Felix. He landed his heel in Felix's chest and knocked him to the ground. Felix was pinned to the carpet, each arm stuck under one of Jimmy's knees, the lamp cord at his throat. They stared at each other, frozen in position.

Felix watched Jimmy's expression melt. Their faces were a breath apart. Jimmy looked down, inspecting the position he was in. Shocked, he hopped up and dropped the lamp cord.

The door swung open. Felix's mother popped her head round.

"Everything all right up here, boys?"

They looked at each other. Jimmy was shaking but trying not to show it. Felix was still on the floor, but he picked up his head and shot a huge smile at the room.

"Fine, Mum, thanks. Fantastic, actually." He beamed. "Totally amazing." A tense laugh escaped from his throat.

"Great. Give me a shout if you need anything." She backed out, and they heard her padding down the stairs. Jimmy couldn't move. He was still humming with the gentle throb of power. He had attacked his best friend. The strength inside him had never sprung on him so quickly before.

"That," Felix said very slowly, "was *so* cool."

"I could have killed you," whispered Jimmy, but Felix didn't take any notice.

"How did you move so fast? And how did you get so strong? I couldn't move. I tried to, but you had me totally stuck. That was amazing!"

"That was dangerous," Jimmy said, quivering again. "What did you do that for? If you throw a lamp at me, then I need to defend myself. I could have done anything, and you could be dead."

"But you didn't kill me, did you? You stopped."

"So? It was lucky." Jimmy dropped the lamp onto the bed and backed away. "Look," he announced, "I don't want to mess about anymore."

"I'm serious, Jimmy," Felix said intently. "What stopped you from killing me just then?"

"I don't know—it was just self-defense. There was no need to kill you, was there? You're just a kid. Like me."

"But it means that you can control it. It's not just an ability to fight. You need to practice."

"I need to hide; until they stop looking for me."

"What if they don't stop? They've taken your parents—don't you want to get them back?"

When Felix said it, it sounded so simple. "If the police aren't going to do it, you have to go and rescue them yourself. You have to use your powers to get your family back." His mouth was twitching impatiently, like a drunken worm rambling across his face.

"You're being ridiculous." Jimmy grew sadder by the second. "I don't even know where they went, or who took them."

"What about Georgie?"

"What about her?"

"Where is she?"

Jimmy hesitated, then gave the obvious answer: "I have no idea."

That night Jimmy couldn't sleep. Every time he closed his eyes, he saw a green stripe on the back of a car, or the face of Sergeant Atkinson. He got up and sat by the window with a glass of water. His nose held back the net curtain and pressed up against the cold glass. One eye could see outside and the other just looked straight into the cloudy haze of the curtain. Really that meant that he couldn't see anything, especially when his breathing steamed up a circle the size of his face.

However he looked at the situation, it was up to him to do something.

Jimmy was pulled out of his thoughts by a soft shuffling at the door.

"Hey," whispered Felix softly. Jimmy turned round and wiped the condensation off his nose.

"Hey," he said.

"Can't sleep?"

"No. You?"

"No." Felix jumped up onto the bed and gently bounced himself into comfort. "Listen, I've had an idea."

"About what?"

"About how to find out what's happening without you having to do it all yourself."

"Cool. What is it?"

"If the police aren't on our side, then we need to find other grown-ups—"

"Who?" Jimmy turned back to the window.

"Important people. People who are on our side."

"We don't know any important people."

"That's what I thought, but what about our teachers? I'll ask Miss Bennett, and she'll get all the other teachers to help. And they can get all their friends, and then they get their friends—"

"And what? They all search their garden sheds?"

"No, but, I dunno, somebody must know what's going on. And it isn't us, so we just have to ask. The whole world can't be against us."

Jimmy downed the rest of his water. Through the bottom of the glass, Felix looked really funny. It made his freckles the size of pennies.

"All right. What about your parents?"

"I'll get them to ask their friends."

"Like who?"

"I dunno, like, whoever." Felix hopped up onto his feet. "Do you want a cookie?"

"No thanks."

"Don't worry, Jimmy; it's going to be okay." Felix reached into the top pocket of his pajamas and pulled out a chocolate cookie. It looked like it had been there for at least a few days. He munched on it as he danced out of the room, waving just before he pulled the door shut.

Jimmy smiled. It was comforting to think Felix might be right. If you want to find something out, the easiest way is just to ask someone. And if it's something particularly tricky or mysterious, maybe it is a good idea to just ask lots and lots of people.

7

RAID

Jimmy woke up early the next morning even though he wasn't going to school. But even if he'd wanted to, Jimmy couldn't have slept through all the noise Felix made. Once Felix was awake, he was a human hurricane. While Jimmy sat in borrowed pajamas, trying to focus on the back of the cereal box, Felix was loosening his school tie, shoveling down breakfast, tying his shoelace, and gabbling at breakneck speed—all at the same time.

"You can't leave the house, Jimmy. I've decided. But if it's the police, they'll work out you're here soon. Hey, maybe they've caught Georgie and they're torturing her or something. Would she squeal?" Jimmy winced, but Felix blew blithely on. "So we have to move fast. Anyway, you'll need to get back to school eventually or you'll have no education and you'll be stupid and you'll get no job and you'll die 'cause you have no food. I might feed you for a while, but I'm not a charity, Jimmy. Anyway, so I'll get Miss Bennett to sort things out for us. I won't say anything that'll give you away, I won't even mention your name, 'cause in school time you never know who's listening, but I reckon if I get her address we can go round to her house and ask for help tonight. Or maybe my mum could phone her. I'll get her number too. Oh, but you shouldn't use the phone, Jimmy. You're allowed to use my computer. And I'm not sure about the garden. But if you do, Dad says don't mess up the lawn, and obviously don't let the neighbors see you. You can't be too careful. So, cool, see you later."

And he was out the door.

"I didn't get it." It seemed like Felix had been gone for days. "I didn't get it," he said again as he kicked off his shoes. "She was so annoying."

"Did you tell her what it was for?" Jimmy said, following Felix into the kitchen.

"Of course not. Too dangerous. That wasn't the plan." Jimmy wasn't too clear about what Felix's plan was, but it was comforting that somebody had a plan. "It's okay," Felix continued. "We'll go and get it."

"What?"

"They must have her address at school, so we'll have to break in and get it."

"Can't we just look her up in the phone book?"

"We don't know her first name, do we? There'll be thousands of Bennetts." Felix dropped his voice slightly as his mother steamed into the room.

"Don't ruin your dinner," she said with a tick of her head. She picked up a magazine and slipped out again.

Felix leaned forward to conspire with Jimmy. "Did they

come after you today?"

"No, nothing happened. I just, well . . ."

"Good." Felix starting fixing two plates of snacks. "We should do it tonight, after Mum and Dad are in bed. This might be our last chance."

"Felix, we can't break into the school and steal Miss Bennett's address. That's criminal."

"Who you gonna call? The police?" Felix had a point. He pushed one of the plates into Jimmy's hands and sat at the table.

"Don't you think this is all a bit, sort of, extreme?" said Jimmy through a mouthful of shortbread cookie. "And even if we manage to break into the building, it's not as if they'll have a box marked 'Staff Addresses' waiting for us, is it?"

"Jimmy, if I were you, I'd be testing out what other amazing things I could do. And if you can learn to control it, to use your strength whenever you like, well, then it would help."

"Can't we at least ask your parents?"

"What?" Felix leaned forward. "Since when were you so pathetic? First of all, I reckon my mum doesn't even believe you. She thinks your mum and dad just aren't answering the phone, or something. She thinks you just don't want to go to school."

At that moment the toaster popped. Jimmy hadn't even noticed him put bread in it. "Toast?" said Felix.

When Felix's father arrived home later, he said he'd been to Jimmy's house and it was empty. Jimmy had hoped that at least Georgie would have found her way back by now, even if his parents hadn't. He came very close to asking Felix's father what they should do. He was such a kind man, and Jimmy loved just hearing his voice. It was a rich, deep sound that bounced round any room he was talking in. Whatever he said, Jimmy found it comforting.

As it turned out, Jimmy didn't need to say anything. Neil Muzbeke explained that he was going to make discrete inquiries at work. "A whole family can't just disappear," he said. Then he started moaning about new police powers, but Jimmy just ate his dinner and let the man's voice soothe him like a hot bath.

It sounded like Neil had the same idea as Felix. If you ask as many people as you can, eventually somebody will know something. It made sense. And it gave Jimmy a little more confidence in Felix's scheme to break into the school.

"We're not doing anything wrong, so stop moaning," Felix hissed. "We're just going to find out Miss Bennett's address." The boys were ready now and stepped back to look at each other. Felix had lent Jimmy some black clothes; they had even found a couple of old balaclavas to put over their heads. Nothing quite fit, but it probably didn't matter.

Felix smirked, but he was trying to focus on their task, so he continued, "There's nothing valuable there, so we're not stealing. We just need to find out her address, then go and visit her."

"Okay, you're right. Let's go."

They blundered downstairs a little too noisily and piled on their coats. Felix turned to Jimmy and gestured at him to be quiet. They had spent all the time since dinner making plans, going over all the scenarios they could think of, and then acting the charade of going to bed. As long as they were back before they were missed, everything would be fine.

Felix pulled the front door shut with a click. Jimmy turned to face the world. He hadn't left the house for two days. Something pricked him inside. Was he just tense, or was that his sense of danger waking up again? He looked at Felix, and they both smiled nervously.

Their first problem was how to get to school. Their usual bus didn't run so late at night, so they had to walk. They set off quickly, swinging their balaclavas by their sides. Neither boy spoke, which was rare for Felix. They had already run through all the possibilities they could think of: alarms, locks, fences. They didn't have any tools with them for cutting through wires or anything. They had decided together that they should travel light; they would probably need to make a quick getaway.

The plan was simple: climb over the fence, then get into the office through the window. They knew this would probably set off an alarm, but as they were only looking for one address, they wouldn't need long. By the time anybody responded, they figured, they'd have found what they needed and be gone.

Jimmy looked across at Felix. There was no smile on his face, and Jimmy realized this was probably more frightening for his friend than it was for him. After all, Jimmy had already spent one long night running through these same streets. That had been far scarier than this: on his own, being chased by a host of faceless characters.

He threw a nervous punch at Felix's arm and giggled.

"What?" snapped Felix, vaguely annoyed.

"Nothing. This is fun, that's all."

At the school gates they paused. It looked very different in the dark. Simultaneously, they pulled their balaclavas over their heads. Jimmy's smelled terrible. It made his face hot, and the wool was itchy. It was necessary, though: anonymity pulled on like an old sock.

The fence was hardly an obstacle. A security light flashed on, but they just jogged past, and waited until it turned itself off. They knew exactly where the office was. In a flash they were at the window. Jimmy instinctively held his wrist where the glass had stuck into him last time he broke a window.

"Give me your coat," he whispered. Felix immediately understood why and whipped it off. He looked even funnier than Jimmy now—his gangly frame shivering in the cold, a black knitted tea cozy over his head.

Jimmy held the coat up against the pane, turned away, and waved to Felix to stand back. *Bang!* His elbow slammed against the coat. That hurt. It sent reverberations up Jimmy's whole arm, but the window wasn't broken. He rubbed his elbow, disgruntled, and threw the coat at Felix's feet.

Felix picked it up. "I'll hold it," he said.

Jimmy used his other arm this time, but still he merely bounced off, more shattered himself than the glass. He just didn't have the strength.

"Let's use a rock," Felix said, pulling his coat back on. He scurried off to look along the grass verge for a big enough stone. Jimmy shook his head, disappointed. The other night he had been powerful, instinctively able to call on amazing skills. What had changed? Now he couldn't even break a window. It should have been easy: so many people did it so often with soccer balls without even meaning to.

He glared at the window and took a couple of steps back. As he did so, he caught sight of something in the reflection. A shadow out of place. Something swaying—but there was no breeze. Jimmy froze. He looked deeper into the glass, trying to focus on the reflection, not the office inside.

"Felix?" he whispered into the night. Every part of him was on edge. He was definitely being watched, but couldn't put his finger on how he knew. Jimmy moved as slowly as he could toward the building until he was up against the wall. Suddenly he heard footsteps coming round from the back of the school. He shrank into the shadows. Someone's outline was cast long onto the playground. It was too late to run now. Jimmy heard the scuffle of steady footsteps on gravel. He held his breath as the silhouette came straight toward him.

"Found one!" It was Felix. "But you should keep your voice down. I could hear you whispering from all the way round the back."

Jimmy breathed once more. "Oh, Felix, I thought—"

He didn't finish his sentence. From nowhere, dozens of men were climbing the fence. Like spiders scaling their webs, they scurried upward. Black against the street lighting, their limbs moved rhythmically and fast. One over the other, so quick. The fence shook with their weight. Felix froze in awe, but Jimmy wasn't hanging around. He couldn't—that incomprehensible energy hit him so hard it almost knocked him off his feet.

Bam!

His elbow smashed through the window with a jerk. The night was filled with a thousand screaming bells. Felix staggered backward.

"What did I get the stone for?" he muttered, but Jimmy had already leaped through the window into the office. He ducked below the windowsill. An instant later, Jimmy's arm reached back out over the glass. He grabbed the back of Felix's coat. In one sweeping move, he lifted the boy off his feet and pulled him through the jagged hole.

"Shhh. Get down!" he hissed. Then, without thinking, he plunged his whole body at the nearest filing cabinet. It crashed to the floor. The locks broke, and the drawers slid open, spilling papers across the floor.

"Wait," said Felix. "I've got it."

He was behind the desk, rifling through a box of record cards marked "Staff Addresses." Jimmy shook his head in disbelief. There was no more time, though. They heard the smash of the front door of the school. Worse, there was a man in the window. A light attached to the side of his head flashed round the room. Faceless, all in black combat gear, he pounded his way over the broken glass. His giant limbs looked like they could have embraced the whole building.

Felix scrunched up the card in his hand and threw it to Jimmy, who caught it. Then Felix zipped to the door. Jimmy's head was pounding. Inside, there was panic, but it wasn't like normal panic. It felt as if it was encased in a soft ball, neutered, so it couldn't get anywhere. His whole body was responding to shrewd and calculated instruction, coming lightning fast from his gut. The intruder spread his arms wide to stop Jimmy from getting to the window. The door slammed shut behind Jimmy, and above the alarm he heard Felix's sneakers squeaking in the hallway. It sounded like a trapped mouse.

In a flash, Jimmy dropped to the floor and slid under this huge man. He stopped himself by grabbing hold of a pile of papers from the fallen filing cabinet. With his other hand, he scooped up some of the broken glass as he got to his feet and flung it in the air behind him. It showered the man, forcing him to shield his eyes as he tried to follow Jimmy.

Jimmy made it outside. He pulled off his balaclava and let the air beat his face as he ran to the fence.

Felix was still wearing his balaclava. He legged it down the hall as fast as he could, but it was no good. They were coming toward him from the other direction too. Still the alarm wailed. No one was in sight yet, but there were shadows and voices. Doors slammed. The place was infested. He stopped, spun round, then cursed himself for thinking so slowly. They had him.

Two men, both big and both all in black. Felix couldn't feel his knees, he was so scared. He couldn't move. He was done for, certainly. Images of prison flooded his head, his parents weeping, him as an old man being released to work as a dish-washer. Still, nothing happened. Why hadn't they pounced?

Then he heard one of them. "Where is he? Which way did he go?"

Slowly, Felix realized they were talking to him. He pulled himself up to his full height, which wasn't tall enough by far. He looked up into the two faces, all blacked out. With excite-ment rising up inside him, he realized they had mistaken him for one of their squad—he was all in black too. They were look-ing for Jimmy, and they weren't expecting any other kids to be there. Felix cleared his throat and dropped the pitch of his voice as low as it would go.

"Hum," he grunted, "down there." He pointed back down the hall.

"Hey, do you meet the minimum height requirement?" said

one of the men as they strode past. The other one dug him in the ribs.

"Shhh, how offensive is that? C'mon, let's get the boy."

"Sorry, but, you know . . . ," and they broke into a run.

Felix couldn't believe his luck. He laughed and shouted out after them: "I'm special division!"

His laughter was cut off by a massive crash from outside. Felix lunged into one of the classrooms and looked out of the window. A police car had burst through the school gates. Behind it stood a line of policemen, and they all sprinted in. If they were still looking, Felix thought, that meant they didn't have Jimmy. He squeezed up his face and fists, wishing for his friend to get away.

Outside it was chaos. The policemen were talking to one of the biggest of the men in black. Everybody was hurrying about, shouting into walkie-talkies. Felix took a deep breath. He marched into the hall, then strolled to the front of the building as casually as he could. At the front door of the school he saw a whole troop of the black-clad raiders. He steered clear of them, and instead picked on a policeman.

"Hey you!" Felix shouted in his gruffest voice. The officer looked shocked.

"Me?"

"Me, *sir*!" Felix corrected him.

"Yes, sir!" The policeman saluted.

"What's going on here?" Felix was starting to sound like his father. "I have a whole unit trying to secure the area, and you lot make that mess." He marched on as he babbled, amazed that he was fooling them. The policeman followed him to the gate, making wretched apologies. "Sort it out. Who has the keys to this vehicle? Find him!"

They passed the police car, but Felix didn't stop. The policeman dashed off, and Felix kept moving: out of the gates, along the sidewalk, shouting more meaningless orders to the policeman waiting there, along the street, round the corner. And then he ran. He ran as hard as he could until he couldn't breathe.

He staggered on, bent double, then ran some more. Pulling off his coat and balaclava, fighting with his sweater, still reeling onward, Felix made it home. The key shook in his hand. He burst through the front door and froze.

In front of him was the sight he had least wanted: his parents. They fixed him with two killer stares.

"Where have you been?" his mother screamed.

"And where's Jimmy?" said his father.

NEVER SAFE

Jimmy had made it outside, but only as far as the playground. His hair was squashed into a bowl shape, with just a tuft sticking up at the back. Sweat stuck to him all round his head and neck. He stuffed the papers in his hands into the pockets of his coat. The alarm still rang out, but now it was joined by sirens. Jimmy glanced behind him. Out of the window came the man he had just peppered with glass. No time to move. As the man leaped out, Jimmy's foot sprang up behind him. A powerful kick landed right in the man's middle, and he crumpled. Now all the other attackers were converging on Jimmy.

Turning like a dancer, nimble on his feet, he jumped onto the windowsill, reached for the top of the window, and pulled himself up. Clambering upward, he was four meters off the ground in a flash. Everyone was watching, the flashlights on their heads intersecting on Jimmy.

He strained his arms and swung from one second-floor window ledge to the next, clutching onto tiny cracks in the old brickwork as he went, his fingers turning white with the pressure. He was round the side of the building now, face against the wall, but he could feel the lights scorching into the back of his head. Suddenly, they flicked upward. Following the intense beams, Jimmy saw three ropes falling from the roof like flying snakes. Figures appeared at the top of each rope, and Jimmy heard the swish of three rappellers sweeping down toward him. As one, they juddered to a halt at Jimmy's level. He was trapped.

In an instant, Jimmy realized why his body had told him to climb. A band of men was clustered below him, in front of the school's perimeter fence—but behind that was a chance.

Bending his knees, Jimmy let go with his hands and slowly tipped backward. Surely this is impossible, he thought, even as he could feel himself doing it. Then, at the critical point, he pushed out with his legs.

The thrust sent him flying backward into the air. Facing upward, he couldn't see the ground, or the men below following him with their gaze, amazed and impotent. Jimmy stretched out his hands. His fingers locked onto the cold wire of the fence. With the grace of a gymnast, his feet swung upward until they were directly above his hands. Jimmy was vertical and upside down, in a perfect handstand on the top of the fence.

Then the momentum pushed him onward, and he pivoted. He scrunched up his face as he came crashing into the other side of the fence. For an instant, he was eye to eye with an openmouthed soldier, but the wire mesh was between them. Letting go, Jimmy dropped to the ground and landed on his feet. He smiled into the soldier's flashlight beam as if he were at the dentist, and ran.

By the time the squad cars were in a position to go, Jimmy was nowhere to be seen.

Alone in the night again.

This was meant to be easy, he thought. Just get there, break the window, and get out with the address. That's what Felix had said. Jimmy mocked the words as they revolved in his head. He felt like an idiot for going along with such an obviously stupid plan. From now on, he thought, I'm only doing what I decide to do. But then he remembered that he didn't even have full control of himself. There was that something inside him, always waiting to take over. And it was getting more powerful. Jimmy didn't need Felix to get him into trouble—he was perfectly capable of doing that himself.

Poor, misguided Felix. One by one, the people closest to Jimmy were being cut away—his parents, his sister, and now his best friend. Would he see any of them again?

A sob rose in his chest and he slumped against a mailbox. The red paint was dulled by the starless sky and fake orange light. He closed his eyes for a second, as if he were looking for something inside his own head. Was he really himself again? Or was there still something else controlling him, moving him, thinking for him? It was getting harder to tell.

He reached into his coat pockets and unscrunched their contents. First was the record card that Felix had thrown him: Miss Bennett's address. He stared at the typed letters, and his eyes sparked with surprise. Miss Bennett lived just around the corner from his house—the house he was beginning to think he might never return to. He pushed the thought down as soon as he felt it.

There was rain in the air now. A light spray that mixed with Jimmy's sweat and softened the paper in his hands. He was still holding what he had grabbed from the floor of the school office—end-of-term reports for most of his grade.

He flicked through, picturing the faces to go with the names he knew, wondering whether he'd see them again. Only one report was intended for him: from Mr. Chase, his PE teacher. Just the week before, Jimmy had refused to go into the swimming pool, so the report was damning. Jimmy just hated splashing around in the water, gasping for air, and didn't see why he had to do it. At first he almost smiled—this was one report that would never make it home. Then another wave of sadness hit him; school seemed a lifetime away.

Jimmy pushed himself off the pavement and wiped his hand on his trousers. How strange that he found himself longing for a normal school day. He let the pages slip from his fingers, and they drifted away in the breeze as he ran on.

Once more Jimmy found himself stepping gently up a front path and ringing someone's bell in the middle of the night. Miss Bennett's house was surprisingly large. Jimmy hadn't known what to expect, but this was bigger than his own family house.

She was a pretty woman, Miss Bennett, and younger than most of Jimmy's teachers. She was also one of the most popular: kind, fair, but strict enough to stand no nonsense. She was always smartly and stylishly dressed. Even now, when she answered the door to Jimmy, she looked calm and composed, her long brown hair tumbling over her shoulders. She stood, statuesque, in a white satin bathrobe.

"Jimmy Coates," she said. "You'd better come in."

He followed her into the kitchen, taking in the dark rooms, all utterly neat, spotlessly clean. Pretty soon Jimmy's fingers were warming around a mug of hot chocolate, but that didn't stop them from shaking.

"Did you cut yourself?" said Miss Bennett. Jimmy ran a finger along the deep gash in his wrist. It hadn't healed, but it had never hurt.

"Yeah, I did," he said, realizing that Miss Bennett would assume he meant accidentally.

When Jimmy had explained, yet again, the story of what had happened to him, including his most recent escape, Miss Bennett nodded, unfazed. She looked all over Jimmy's dirty face, then eventually spoke.

"You haven't said why you think these people are after you." Jimmy didn't answer. He didn't know what to say. Miss Bennett continued, "If you can work out what you have done that might make someone chase you, then we can work out who these people are."

"Well, I think it must be to do with what I can do."

"All your amazing new skills?" she said, one eyebrow creeping up. "You know, Jimmy, the body is capable of remarkable things when put under pressure. Have you heard of adrenaline?" Jimmy didn't answer. "Look, I'm also worried about your parents being stolen away, and your sister running off, so I'll help you. I'll ask the other teachers if they know anything, but I think you shouldn't mention it to anyone else."

"Why not?"

"Well, if you don't know who these people are, you don't know who might be on their side. Who knew you were going to school tonight, for example?"

"Nobody, just me and Felix, and, well, his mum might have heard us; I don't know."

"It sounds like someone knew you were coming, doesn't it? Listen, you can stay here for a while if you like. It's not much fun, but it'll be safe."

"Thanks, but I'll be okay at Felix's. His parents might be worried if they wake up and we're both gone. At least if I'm there, then I can explain that Felix is probably in prison."

"I'm sure his parents knew it was coming sooner or later."

Miss Bennett got up and went into the living room, leaving the door open. She picked up the phone and called out, "I'll call you a cab. What's the address?" Jimmy took a sip of hot chocolate, burning his tongue, then told her.

"Felix, you're here!" It was very late, but when Jimmy knocked on the door, it was Felix who answered, and everybody was up. They were sitting in the kitchen, and Jimmy could tell he had walked in on an argument.

"I thought you'd been arrested."

"I thought you were dead," Felix offered back, deadpan.

Neil and Olivia Muzbeke had only blank faces when Jimmy smiled at them sheepishly. "I'm sorry," he murmured. "It was my fault."

"Oh, Jimmy, come here." Felix's mother stretched out her arms and hugged him so tightly he almost got crushed. It was a while since Jimmy had been hugged like that.

Felix's father let out a gruff sigh. "We were worried about you, Jimmy," he said in his bass voice. "Felix told us what happened. Can you leave things to us from now on?"

Jimmy pulled away from the embrace and looked down at his feet. "I went to see Miss Bennett. She's going to help too."

"Brilliant! Nice one." Felix was punching the air.

"Felix! Calm down and go to bed."

"Yes, Mum." He winked at Jimmy and pretended to sulk while he left the room. When he got to the door, though, it opened for him and let in a tremendous whine. The room was shaking, and the noise grew louder. Then a plate fell off the counter and shattered on the floor.

"What's going on?" Olivia whimpered. "What's happening?"

"Did you call the police?" yelled Jimmy. Felix spun round.

"Mum, you promised you wouldn't! You promised!" he shouted. There was a huge amount of noise now, a loud screeching over the top of a deep whir. Felix's father got up and clutched the back of his chair. He shouted across the table to his wife.

"Did you call the police, Olivia?"

"No, I . . . ," she squeaked, but didn't finish her sentence.

Jimmy ran round the table and looked out of the window. The back garden was empty, but all the plants were completely flattened by an immense wind. Then they were hit by a spotlight. It flooded the whole back garden with white light and streamed into the kitchen.

"Get out of here, Jimmy; out the front." Felix was calm as he spoke, but held his hand up to his eyes to protect them from the light.

Jimmy smiled. "Thanks, Felix," he said. "I'll see you soon," and he strode out of the kitchen. As he breezed through the door, he heard Felix's mother shouting.

"Who are they?" she screamed. "Who are these people?" Jimmy ducked into the living room, which looked out onto the street. Leaving the light off, he crawled across the carpet to the window and gently pulled aside a corner of the curtain. There were floodlights washing the front of the house as well. Jimmy saw cars filling the street—black cars, forming a blockade.

Hordes of black-clad men came streaming out, ducking down and holding their jackets against the swirling wind. Some of them were in suits; some of them were in combat gear, like the men at the school had been. This time they had guns. Huge rifles, with long thin barrels, all pointing straight at the house. Then Jimmy saw the marks on the cars—a thin green stripe on each one. In his head, Jimmy echoed the cry of Felix's mother: Who are these people?

Jimmy crawled back from the window, and as he did he was relieved to feel his insides welling up. His tiredness was scrunched into a ball and flicked away; on came the strength. He was relying on whatever this was to save him. Now he needed it more than ever.

He turned to the window again as he crawled out of the room. There they were, just what he had been expecting since he'd seen the plants blown flat in the garden: two small helicopters swooped like wasps. They hovered at the height of the houses for a second, swaying steadily, their runners sticking out like claws. Then one of them pulled back and up, hovering in position above the house opposite. Its bright eye glared down into the living room. The other one veered off to one side and floated down. It landed in the street, squeezed into the road where there was only just enough space. Jimmy gulped.

He ran back into the hallway, where all three Muzbekes were standing, mystified.

"Get down!" Jimmy shouted at them. "You two—on the floor. Felix, come with me." They sprinted up the stairs together and into Felix's room.

"I told you to run for it," Felix said.

"There's no chance I'll make it. But you can help me."

"Jimmy, they have guns. You're going to get shot."

Jimmy looked around, thinking fast.

"Listen, I don't know how I know"—he looked into Felix's face and saw fear where there was usually a smile—"but I think they're tranquilizer guns."

"What?"

"The barrels are long and thin, not like normal rifles, and somehow I know. I think they just have darts in them to knock me unconscious."

"You mean you *hope* they just have darts in them."

"No, they could have killed me at the school. They had a clear view. It would have been an easy shot."

"What are you saying?"

The noise outside wasn't letting up. Jimmy felt himself smile, but pushed it back. "They want me alive."

Outside, the troops took up their positions, crouching behind the knee-high front wall. They were itching to raid the house. Some pointed guns at the front door, others at the windows.

"Don't take any chances," a voice boomed out of a megaphone. "We know what he's capable of. If you get a clear shot, use it. Take him down."

They waited. The helicopter's rotor kept spinning, and the

one in the air kept its light nailed to the house. The back garden was full of men now, steadily crawling toward the house on their stomachs.

Suddenly, the front door burst open. Their target ran out with his arms up around his face and a baseball cap covering his head. Jimmy's coat billowed in the wind, just like it had when he jumped off the side of the school. He got halfway across the front garden—only about two meters—when a soft splat spit a dart into his neck. He staggered two more steps, but darkness hit him. He fell first to his knees, then onto his front.

A man ran out to the unconscious body. He was cautious, leading with his rifle. When he got close he knelt down. He lifted his left hand off the gun and flipped the boy over.

Another shout over the megaphone: "Do we have an ID?"

He stared into the face looking up at him from the grass. Then he peeled the cap off the boy's head. The man opened his palm. On the inside of the glove on his left hand, just above his wrist, there was a fuzzy picture of Jimmy. Drizzle spattered the plastic cover. He looked from the face to the picture and sprang up.

"Negative!" he shouted, but no one could hear him. He waved frantically and shook his head. "Negative!" he screamed again. He looked along the line of marksmen with their rifles pointing at the house. There was something behind them. A shadow in a coat that didn't fit was sprinting down the road. He turned back to the house: the window of the living room was smashed. Then he turned back to the boy lying on the grass. Felix was smiling, his eyes closed.

"There! Quick!" the man shouted. He pointed first, then took aim with his rifle, but he was too slow, and Jimmy was running too fast. The whole team spun round, shocked to see their target getting away from them.

Jimmy bounced from side to side to avoid the darts that flew past his ear. He heard them whistling by, too close for comfort. He would never make it down the road to the corner. There were at least twenty people chasing him, firing at him, and then he heard the revving of car engines. There was only one way to escape.

The helicopter was sitting not far ahead, everything still spinning. If Jimmy could just make it that far . . . But the pilot was still in the cockpit. He watched Jimmy get closer. Through the drizzle he saw the glint in his eyes and knew what Jimmy was going to try to do. The pilot set about the controls, and the rotor picked up pace. The humming got louder, deafening Jimmy as he ran into the wind. The helicopter smoothly lifted its feet off the asphalt, but there wasn't much room to maneuver. It was small, but it had still taken a skillful landing to get it into this enclosed space, and now it couldn't just zoom away.

The wind slowed Jimmy down, but his legs were strong, and they kicked out harder than ever. Darts pinged into the metal of the machine in front of him, missing him by a whisker. Was it the wind or fortune that sent them off course?

At last Jimmy was close enough. He leaped forward, and as the helicopter surged upward, he caught a runner with both hands. The helicopter dipped with his weight, but Jimmy's feet didn't hit the ground. Rain, grease, and sweat made his grip slippery, and the darts kept coming at him until he was well above the level of the houses. The pilot looked into Jimmy's face with a mixture of anger and panic. He was screaming into his microphone.

Jimmy arched his chin up and hooked it over the runner, then his right elbow, then his left. The nose of the helicopter jerked down, and the whole thing banked away from Jimmy. He could only just hold on and he slammed against the underside of the aircraft. Then the pilot tore the joystick the other way, rocking the helicopter in midair.

The slipstream hacked into Jimmy's limbs, but he was equal to it. He strained himself up with even more force, determination contorting his face. Then he flung his right leg to one side and hooked his foot over the runner. From there, he launched himself into the cockpit.

Although he was half the size of the pilot, Jimmy seemed to have twice the strength. He ripped off the man's helmet and heaved him over the side. For a split second the pilot gazed up at the heavens, before bouncing off a rooftop into a tree.

Rain speckled the glass, then blew straight off it again. The force of the wind from the rotor created its own tornado. Jimmy was sitting at the center of it. The helmet was too big for him and kept slipping back onto his neck, or over his face, covering his eyes. It had a microphone attached to it, which curled round and hit him on the nose, and headphones built into it, which shut out most of the sound. His head was buzzing with more than noise, though. He was alone in an airborne helicopter. He gulped again, and realized there probably wasn't an instruction manual at hand.

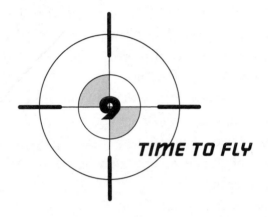

9
TIME TO FLY

Jimmy stared at the controls in front of him: switches, lights, dials, computer displays, and a heavy joystick. They stretched back over his head and all around him, as if he could control five helicopters from here—plus a dishwasher, a TV, and a microwave. There were four switches in a row just to his left, with a picture of a rocket above each one; there was a small, circular computer screen that flicked between different read-outs. Most noticeable of all, in a small space on the control panel, about the width of the switches, was a green stripe.

While Jimmy was blinking at the dazzling controls around him, the machine tipped from side to side in the wind. Then it started to dive. Any minute Jimmy would come crashing to the ground in a snarling mess of metal. Like a pebble into a pond, the helicopter plummeted.

Slowly, though, the labyrinth of controls started to make sense. It was like a dim memory coming back to him. Jimmy recognized the strange, cut-diamond shape of the aircraft;

phrases like *engine torque* and *magnetic heading* flooded his mind. Then his fingers started buzzing, warming as the blood flowed through them again. Before Jimmy even noticed, they were dashing about the controls. The helicopter stopped juddering, and Jimmy's hands curled round the joystick. He knew how to fly. He didn't know how he knew, but he knew—just like he had known about the guns. The whole weight of the helicopter shifted beneath him. He was up in the sky again.

Twin LHTEC-950 turboshaft engines; five-blade, bearingless main rotor; FANTAIL anti-torque system—Jimmy's head spun with a million technical terms. He didn't just know how to fly, he knew he was in a PAH-62 Comanche, product of the world's most advanced aerospace technology.

Jimmy looked at the computer screen. It was showing a full-color simulation of the helicopter and everything around it. Unfortunately, there wasn't just one helicopter on the screen. There was another one behind it—too close.

Jimmy brought the chopper lower in the sky, swooping over the rooftops, skimming the TV aerials and satellite dishes. The buildings were getting taller now, and in the distance Jimmy recognized the spectacular view of London's Docklands. At breakneck speed he dipped and dove between skyscrapers that grew up as northeast London became central London. Still the other helicopter kept up with him.

As he reached the river, Jimmy zoomed down, as low as he could. The runners skimmed the top of the water, and Jimmy had to dodge the rusty barges and the late-night boats full of drunken partygoers. The relentless whisk of the rotor threw water up around him on all sides. The other helicopter was right behind now, and started closing the gap.

They zipped along the Thames as if it were a racetrack. Jimmy kept low, but Tower Bridge zoomed toward him. Behind, the other helicopter pulled up to skip over the top of it, but Jimmy surged forward and whirred between the bridge and the water. There was barely enough space. For a moment, Jimmy could hear the echo of the metalwork crests rattling around him.

Jimmy had opened up a small lead now, but that wasn't good enough. He wasn't trying to win a race; he had to completely lose his pursuer. He carried on like a supersonic arrow, buzzing under and over the bridges. With a smile interrupting his face, Jimmy started reveling in the speed and in the control. It didn't matter how close they got, he thought. He knew they couldn't fire their rockets at him because they wanted him alive. Then he had an idea.

Jimmy pulled the helicopter higher, skimming over the next bridge, then shook his helmet off into his hand. He bent the microphone round the joystick and jammed the helmet between it and the panel of switches. It held the joystick at a set angle, with the helicopter climbing very slightly but steadily. Jimmy glanced over the side into the water. For all his new skills, he still hated the idea of swimming.

He touched the computer screen, and a target circle appeared. With his finger he carefully moved it to a point in the water up ahead of him. Then with a bold flick, he clicked two of the rocket switches. All of a sudden, the lights on the control panel started flashing, and he felt the Comanche rumbling. Two ropes of flame twisted through the air in front of him. They avoided the next bridge, one above it and one below it, then dove into the river.

Up ahead Jimmy could see the glorious sight of the Houses

of Parliament and the London Eye on opposite banks, both illuminated. But there was no time to enjoy them—after a second underwater, the rockets exploded. They sent a massive sheet of water high up into the air, completely obscuring Jimmy's view. Hopefully it would do the same to the helicopter behind him.

Checking that the joystick was secure, he threw himself over the side. He just let his feet part company with the floor of the cockpit, while the helicopter carried on upward, empty. The other one blindly followed it—two mechanical hawks that dipped past Big Ben and over the horizon. They'd be out to sea by the time his pursuers realized what had happened.

Jimmy fell like a boulder. His insides were heaved upward. His brain spun; his stomach leaped to his throat. He flailed about in the air, falling faster and farther than he ever would have expected, too stunned to scream.

Smack!

He hit the water, and the world shifted into slow motion. His legs crumpled with the impact; a crash landing like that, even on water, should have broken bones. Jimmy's mind threw up images of him landing on concrete in the driveway of his house. It wasn't the fall that was going to harm him.

Through shock, his lungs snatched one last gulp of air before he went under. It was cold—so cold. It shuddered through him like an electric pulse. For an agonizing moment he couldn't move his arms or legs. The air that billowed in his coat slowed him down, but he couldn't trap it in. As the bubbles fluttered up, Jimmy sank faster. He felt like a fool now, for jumping into the water—a drowning fool.

Looking up, none of the vague shapes seeping through the water meant anything to him. The night was too dark and the water too thick with mud for him to be able to see anything except indistinct shadows. Even they were disappearing rapidly, the deeper he went. His breath was going too. How long had he been under? Thirty seconds? Fifty? Longer? He plummeted to the bottom of the Thames.

Everything around him was black. His lungs were ticking off the seconds, but his arms and legs shook into action. Jimmy hated swimming, but now he was in the water and he didn't have a choice. The blood started gently warming his arms and legs as they kicked out. He had to get to the surface; he had to breathe.

His legs felt strong, and Jimmy wasn't panicking. His muscles were operating on their own. Then his arms reached out, and his whole body started moving as if he had always been a swimmer. But it was a long way back up to the surface, and the current wasn't letting up. He couldn't hold his breath anymore. He must have been underwater for over a minute, as much as a minute and a half even. It felt like hours. His lungs were hurting, screaming out for air. His body was kicking, working hard, moving him up; slowly he was making it—but too late.

He couldn't stop himself. The pain in his lungs was sharp and burning. He was still a long way from the air he craved, but his mouth snapped open and his lungs gasped for breath. Water flooded into him. Disgusting, polluted Thames water—and Jimmy knew that meant he would drown.

But he was wrong. He closed his eyes and stopped kicking, but nothing happened. He didn't black out; the burning in his lungs was gone; his head wasn't spinning anymore. Jimmy opened his eyes. He was breathing. Except he was inhaling water.

Life rushed back to every point in his body. His fingers turned from blue back to juicy pink. He was moving with the ease of a killer whale. He flipped his body over and made a dive for the riverbed.

Even in the deep black, Jimmy's eyes began to adjust. He caught glimpses of extraordinary shapes that he made into household objects in his head: fridges, old-fashioned baby carriages, treasure chests—centuries of random rubbish dumped into the Thames.

He glided along the bottom until he found the wall, then followed it up. Gradually, light spread out around him. He was nearly up to the surface when something caught his eye. He wasn't sure, but nestling among the moss and the slime was something on the wall. . . . Jimmy's legs had kicked him away from it by now. Was he imagining things? Or had he seen a green stripe painted on the wall, a stripe the size of himself?

Whoosh!

His head broke through into the air.

He was right by the floating pier, and he stretched out his hand to grab the side. A huge cough brought up two lungfuls of putrid water. He hauled himself up and crawled away onto Westminster Bridge.

He was breathing heavily, his knees clinging to the pavement. He felt the crippling squeeze of being on the run close in around him. It was as if the air itself was trying to catch him. He was still wearing Felix's ill-fitting clothes, but now they were dripping wet, and the night was cold. He vainly pulled his coat tighter around him.

The Thames was quiet. A few confused bystanders reached the banks of the river too late to witness anything. The two small, black helicopters were long gone. The water had settled back to its natural heaving; in a few minutes the boat with the party on it trundled past under him. Jimmy threw an empty smile onto the deck. There was nothing to be happy about. He might have escaped so far, but he couldn't go on running for the rest of his life. He still didn't even know who he was running from.

A bus screeched past. A puddle was forming all around Jimmy, and he stared into it. He sat there waiting to cry, until the water he was sitting on seemed warm. The huge London Eye could have been staring at him. It lumbered round, and when Jimmy looked at it, it made him dizzy, so he looked back down at the stone of the bridge floor. Below him he could see the river, a thick brown, with a slight sparkle bouncing off the surface that reflected London's night lights.

It looked more like the sea than a river. Watching the current made him giddy, so he pulled himself to his feet and leaned over the green copper handrail. From deep inside him he retched up black puke that fell into the water. That's when Jimmy let go of the tears.

Surely anything would be better than this, he thought. Whatever they wanted to do to him—lock him up, experiment on him, put him in the circus—it would have to be better than living on the streets and having to run every time they came for him. A sickness in his heart told him he should give up; it was the weird force inside him that kept him running. He just wished it would go away. Jimmy felt like it was pushing him aside. His real personality was fading out, submerged by this thing inside him.

Had it been him escaping from Felix's house, Jimmy wondered, or the power inside him? For the first time, it was hard to distinguish between the actions he had chosen and the ones that his body had done for him. Which one of them had made the decision to go for the helicopter? He tried to think back, but kept imagining the shot of a gun, and Felix falling to the grass in front of his house.

Jimmy gazed up at the grandeur of the Houses of Parliament and wondered if anybody in there could help him. The gothic spires glowed gold in the night, and Big Ben stretched up like a rocket ready to take off. He closed his eyes and pictured himself in that warm living room watching pictures of the prime minister and that other man his parents were always arguing about. That was the moment his life had started to escape his control.

Morning eventually crept up behind him. A beautiful sunrise licked away the night. When the light started seeping through his eyelids, Jimmy stretched out. The hours leaning against the cold stone of Westminster Bridge had made him stiff. His neck clicked as he rolled it from side to side. He was happy to have made it through another night, the terrible dreams already forgotten. The bridge was busy, even though it was nowhere near nine o'clock. Big Ben struck out the early hour, and traffic screamed past, mainly buses and taxis.

Jimmy was suddenly aware of three things: he was still very wet, he was incredibly hungry, and he was extremely visible. He realized he shouldn't have let himself fall asleep without finding a place to hide first.

"Jimmy!"

He heard his name and automatically huddled himself into a ball, his eyes flitting around anxiously. Whose voice was that? It called his name again. This is it, he thought. They've found me.

DROWNING TWICE

"Jimmy!" The call was closer. This time it stirred something in Jimmy. Not strength, and not fear either, but a warm relief. He knew that voice. He felt a weight fly off his shoulders, and a smile flashed onto his face.

"Georgie!" he shouted with delight as his sister ran toward him. He couldn't believe that he hadn't recognized his sister's voice instantly. She snatched his shivering hand and pulled him up.

"You're okay!" She beamed, then suddenly frowned. "You stink! You didn't fall in the Thames, did you? Have you any idea the diseases you could get?"

Jimmy didn't answer. However much he was amazed at his swimming, he was still relieved to be out of the water. That was one instinct that would take some overcoming.

The sun shone right into his eyes and he squinted up at Georgie. She wasn't alone. Behind her, he could see her best friend, Eva. She waved, slightly embarrassed, and her reddish brown hair flapped around her ears. And who was that—a middle-aged man with a concerned frown around his thick eyebrows? Of course: Eva's father, Stanley Doren.

"Oh, Jimmy, I'm so happy to see you. If you weren't so wet I'd give you a hug." Georgie gingerly kissed him on the cheek, but Jimmy wasn't satisfied with that—he plunged his arms around her, crushing her in a soaking embrace.

In no time they were all on the subway and Jimmy had fallen asleep with his head on Georgie's shoulder. Even the noise of the train and the shouted conversation of the other three couldn't stop him from dropping off. Wet through, and stinking of the river, he had Eva's father's coat on over Felix's to keep him warm. It wasn't really working, but that didn't matter.

It wasn't long before Jimmy saw another spare room, more borrowed pajamas, with another borrowed toothbrush. And yet again he was going to sleep in the middle of the day. He was almost becoming nocturnal.

The Dorens lived in a beautiful house, even larger than the Muzbekes'. It was positively grand. Eva was the youngest of the family, with two much older brothers. They had already gone through university and moved out. Jimmy was in one of the brothers' vacated bedrooms. He didn't know which one. To be honest, he couldn't even remember what they looked like or what their names were, and he didn't care. He needed to make up for the night spent sleeping rough, which had meant hardly sleeping at all.

He woke up with a headache, sure that he'd just had another nightmare, but unable to recall any of it. Eva and Georgie were waiting for him in the kitchen when he eventually got there. He wasn't used to so many rooms, so many different doors and different ways to go. He almost got lost.

Georgie was desperate to know what was going on, but Jimmy was too.

"Where have you been?" Jimmy shot out his question first, quicker on the draw.

"We've been looking for you. Where did you run off to?" said Eva, with a hint of frustration.

"Georgie's the one who ran off. I was under the car."

"Under the car? What were you doing there?" Georgie peered at him as if he were mad.

Jimmy didn't answer. He thought it was pretty obvious he hadn't gone under the car to check the engine.

She carried on, ignoring his silence. "Anyway, I told Eva the whole story: the two men who came for you, the woman who kept me and mum and dad in the living room while you escaped out the window—why did you jump out the window? And why were they after you?"

"They still *are* after me, but I don't know who they are. Did you say the *woman* who kept you in the living room?"

"Yeah; she had a gun. And Mum and Dad knew her, I think. They were surprised to see her."

"But I saw her shoes. She had men's shoes on." Jimmy remembered it clearly—the extra set of feet that he'd seen from under the car. The pattern on them had been distinctive, but they were definitely smart, male, office shoes. And he'd seen them somewhere before.

"What do you know about shoes?" said Eva.

"Whatever," interrupted Georgie. "You have to tell us

everything that happened."

So Jimmy spent a long time running through his story again. Eva's mother, Audrey Doren, even put together some refreshments: tiny sausages on cocktail sticks, and strips of carrot with a pot of something white and weird-looking to dip them in. Jimmy avoided the carrots but was through the sausages in no time. He washed it all down with some orange juice.

He went through his story slowly so that he didn't forget anything. There wasn't much risk of that, though. Most of it he remembered in too much detail for his own liking, and he skipped over many of his own observations. Like the green stripe he thought he'd seen under the Thames—that would have made him sound completely paranoid. He went through from the beginning. It seemed so long ago that he'd been walking through the night with Mitchell.

"So he tried to mug you?" Georgie said.

"Yeah, but it was okay. He turned out to be okay, I mean. He was nice. Actually he reminded me of you, Georgie."

"Why?"

"Well, I don't know. Maybe because he kept calling me an idiot too."

That made everyone at the table laugh except Georgie. "He sounds terrible," she said grumpily, but Eva was still giggling.

"Sounds interesting to me," she said. "Was he fit?"

Jimmy ignored her and carried on until his throat was dry. Just as he got to the end, Eva's mother opened the door with a bang and went to stand at the kitchen counter. It startled Jimmy, who hadn't noticed her slip out.

"Don't you want to hear what I've been doing?" said Georgie.

But Eva broke in. "We've already heard it. Can we go back to school now we've found him?"

"Shut up; I'm going to tell him." So Georgie took a big gulp of orange juice and started rattling off her tale, words tumbling over one another in a rush.

"Well, I wasn't just going to let them take me away, whoever they were. And they had guns. So they had to be bad, right? So I kicked one of them—"

"I saw that," interrupted Jimmy. "I saw all this from under the car."

"Oh, sure; so I ran off down the street, but I don't think anybody followed me." Georgie's mind flashed back to the cold, the surreal glow of the streetlights, feeling lost. "So then, obviously, I ran to the police station. And unlike you, Jimmy, I know where things are. So I went straight there and told Sergeant Anderson—"

"Atkinson?"

"Yes, Sergeant Atkinson. I told him all about it, but he said he knew. He said that they were just waiting for you to turn up. I said that they should go out and look for you, but he said that they already were. And he said something very strange. He said that you were very important to them and that they had to catch you. But he wouldn't say why. Now, I know you, Jimmy, and I know that even though you're an idiot, you wouldn't break the law—"

"Just stick to the story, would you?" Jimmy sighed.

"—I know you wouldn't break the law, even by accident, and you don't have the brains to plan any big crimes." Jimmy wanted to scream but he just didn't have the energy. There hadn't been nearly enough little sausages on sticks. "So I said no thanks, and that I was going. But then he said he couldn't let me leave. They needed me, in order to catch you. So, well, I kicked him in the knee. Then another policeman tried to stop me, so I picked up the fire extinguisher and swung it into his face. Then I ran off."

Jimmy thought back to his trip to the police station: the officer with the bloody face, and Sergeant Atkinson's limp. It all made sense now. He smiled at his sister.

She carried on: "From there I wasn't just going to wander the streets, so I wanted to call someone, tell them to pick me up or whatever, or get a cab. But when I found a pay phone, it was out of order. There were two actually, and they'd both been smashed, which was weird, so I just walked."

"And she came straight here," added Eva.

"Yeah. I came here."

"Oh, ri-right," Jimmy stuttered. "So, what about since you've been here?"

"I dunno," started Georgie. "I tried to think of all the places you could go, but we couldn't find you. . . ."

Eva's father took up the story. "I've been helping the girls look for you, Jimmy. We'd driven round the whole of this area without any luck, then Georgie said something about Westminster Bridge, so we checked there every morning and evening as well."

Jimmy looked at Georgie, a little confused.

"I thought you'd remember about my project," she explained, "and that I'd have to go there eventually. I decided that's where you'd go if you wanted to find me."

Jimmy nodded. He didn't want to disappoint Georgie by telling her he hadn't gone there on purpose. He'd just landed there when he jumped out of the helicopter.

"I didn't even want to do Westminster Bridge," Georgie continued. "It's a stupid topic. But Mum and Dad made me. They insisted." Her smile vanished, and her eyes fell to the floor.

"Still hungry, Jimmy?" Mrs. Doren interjected. "I made another plate of sausages just for you." She put it down in front of him next to another tall glass of orange juice.

"Do you have any Coke?" he asked hopefully, knowing it had become too expensive for most people.

"Well"—she was slightly thrown—"juice is better for you."

"Sure."

It was late afternoon, and it was already getting gray outside. The wind had picked up too, and it whistled round the house and through the expanse of garden that stretched away out the window.

"So, do you think we'll be able to find Mum and Dad?" Jimmy was hesitant, and asking no one in particular. No one made eye contact.

Eventually, Stanley Doren tried to answer. "That's hard to say, Jimmy. Has anyone asked you for money or given you a note?"

"Nobody's given me anything but a hard time."

There was a heavy pause.

"Hey, Jimmy." Georgie broke the silence. "Eva's parents have explained to me about all the stuff on TV that Mum and Dad argue about. It's exactly what I said."

"What?" Jimmy felt a strange sleepiness fill his head. He took another sip of juice to refresh himself.

"You know, why they shout at each other every time the prime minister comes on TV." She looked up at Mrs. Doren.

"Tell him what you told me. I was right."

"You're always right, Georgie." Jimmy tried to sound sarcastic, but there was something wrong. He had started feeling sort of . . . fuzzy.

"All I was saying," started Mrs. Doren as her husband stood up with a sigh and left the room, "was that the prime minister, Ares Hollingdale . . ." The name seeped into Jimmy's head like he'd never heard it before. It threw him, and dizziness swam around his brain. He gripped the table as Mrs. Doren repeated the name.

"Ares Hollingdale has been doing marvelous things. Wonderful things, Jimmy. He's the best prime minister this country has ever had. But, you see, some people don't like the more radical reforms that he's been bringing in." Jimmy was hardly able to listen now, concentrating on staying upright in his chair. "When he came into power, the country was in a mess. You probably don't remember, of course."

Jimmy couldn't even see straight, let alone remember anything. Audrey Doren's voice was flying away, growing distant. ". . . So he's brought in fantastic new measures, like reducing the amount of freedom for people who are going to commit crimes."

Jimmy's sickness spread. People who are *going* to commit crimes? That doesn't make sense. He felt like he was drowning—again.

"These days he runs the country without needing permission from the public or the Palace or the House of Lords or anybody at all, which means decisions are made efficiently, and for the best. It's called neo-democracy, where people only vote when it's appropriate. Otherwise, the PM does it for them."

Jimmy's nausea was spreading down his body. Then, like a kick in the gut, he felt his dark energy powering up, but not like before. It stirred around his stomach, misty and vague. Then it met the nausea coming down from his throat and was swallowed up.

"So probably one of your parents supported Ares Hollingdale, quite rightly, but one of them didn't."

Jimmy went to take the last sip of his orange juice, but couldn't see the glass properly and knocked it over. He slumped onto the table.

"It's for the best, Jimmy. For the good of the country."

Distant, as if it was in a dream, he heard his sister scream. Blackness hit him like a sledgehammer.

38 PERCENT

Bam!

Light smacked into Jimmy's eyes. His body snapped forward so that he was sitting up. His head was pounding harder than ever. For a second he thought he remembered a sliver of a nightmare, but then it was gone. He was sitting on a silver-colored metal table. The room was hot. The only light came from two fluorescent bars hanging from the ceiling. The walls were bare, gray brick. It looked like a bunker of some kind, or a prison. How had he got here? The wall opposite him swam in and out of focus. Jimmy tried to shake the fog from his head. What was the last thing he remembered?

He thought he was alone, but then a voice from behind him interrupted his thoughts. It was a voice he recognized: the deep, kind tones of Sergeant Atkinson. Too kind. His voice was like a deep feather pillow pressed over your face.

"Welcome to NJ7, Jimmy."

Jimmy swung round on the table. The fourth wall of the

room had a small metal door in it. There was no door handle. Sergeant Atkinson was sitting on a plastic chair in the corner, swamping it with his giant body. He leaned forward on one bulging forearm.

"Sergeant Atkinson?"

"It's okay; you don't have to call me that anymore. I'm not a police sergeant. You probably guessed that, though." He sat upright and indicated his uniform. It was a light, crisp blue, like a summer sky, and the trim shone gold. On his chest there was a parade of medals in every bold color under the sun, including a single green stripe. Jimmy blinked faster, as if that would make it disappear.

"My name is Paduk. I'm head of special security for the Neo-democratic State of Britain. This is NJ7." He grinned all the way across his chiseled face, and everything creased up. To Jimmy he looked like some strange blond toad.

"What's NJ7?"

Paduk sprang off his chair, still grinning. He was so tall he had to be careful to duck under the hanging lights.

"NJ7 is the most advanced military intelligence agency in the world."

"If it's that secret, how come you're telling me about it? And what am I doing here?" Jimmy was coming round fast now, his thoughts moving more freely. Before Paduk could answer, the door swung open. Again Jimmy had to blink to make sure what he was seeing was real. In shuffled a small man, hunched over with age, in a coat as white as his skin.

"Mr. Higgins?" said Jimmy with a gasp, staring at his half-deaf next-door neighbor.

"Actually, it's *Dr.* Higgins," was the sharp reply.

"You're Mr. Higgins, from next door!" said Jimmy, louder than he would have spoken to anybody else.

"And you're going to have to listen to things the first time they are said to you, young man. I am *Dr.* Kasimit Higgins. Perhaps you'd like to come with me?" He raised his head in invitation to Jimmy, but also to Paduk, who nodded solemnly.

Still trying to shake off the drumming in his head, Jimmy followed Dr. Higgins. Paduk walked behind them, hunched over through the low corridors. Every now and again, Jimmy could tell by the shadows swinging from side to side in front of him that Paduk had hit one of the overhanging lights with the top of his head. He didn't hear any complaint about it though.

They walked for several minutes along a labyrinth of gray brick corridors. In some places there was a drip of water coming from the ceiling, but nowhere were there any windows. That made Jimmy think they might be underground.

Jimmy's hands wandered about his pockets while he tried to clear his head. His fingers wrapped around something—a pen. Jimmy clutched it tightly. Maybe he could use it as a weapon. This could be his only chance to escape. Behind him was a giant of a man, but he had got past him once before—even Georgie had. Jimmy was certain that he would be able to get out of this place with his strange powers. If he could summon them.

He had to concentrate. Why weren't they springing up on him like every other time he had been in danger? He focused on that area behind his stomach, trying to start it rumbling. Was it there? Was it coming? Something *was* stirring inside him. Faintly at first, then growing—that urgency throbbing between his belly and his ribs.

But if Jimmy did manage to overpower these two men, where would he go? And even if he managed to escape from this weird underground maze now, he would never know what was going on. His desire to find out what had been happening to him, and who had been chasing him, was immense. The feeling inside him stopped and faded to nothing in a second.

Had he willfully pushed it back? Had he even summoned it, or was it coincidence it had risen up just then?

Jimmy couldn't suppress a smile. He had never been able to call it up before, and he felt an unexpected excitement: He had developed some kind of control over his weird power. He had either told it to come, or at the very least, he had told it to go away. He settled himself and carried on the silent walk.

The twisting tunnels continued without a single door. They turned another corner. Now there were noises, faint voices, and then the end of the corridor opened up into another boxlike room. There were desks lining the walls, and a handful of people tapping away at computers, their faces lit by the blue-green light of technical-looking screens.

Keeping his back to Jimmy, Dr. Higgins took a seat at an old-fashioned wooden desk in the center of the room. There was nothing on the leather top except a pen. He sat there for a second while Jimmy and Paduk waited behind him, then turned his head and ushered them round.

"Come on, come on, round here. I can't talk to you if you're behind me, can I?" So Jimmy did as he was told, quite bemused by the old man's attitude. "Did Paduk explain anything to you?"

"Not really. He said something about NJ7, but . . ."

"Ah, NJ7. Congratulations, Jimmy, you are a member of the

finest effects-espionage team in the world."

So many questions sprang up in Jimmy's mind. Nothing was being explained to him very well. He didn't know where to start.

"I am?" he said eventually. But when he heard his meek little voice lost in the bustle of the room, he pulled himself together. If he was ever going to find out what was going on, this was his chance. "What's 'effects espionage'?" he asked, boldly.

"Aha, that's a little concept this government has come up with—this *wonderful* government, I should say; excuse me. Espionage usually means spies rooting around, gathering intelligence. But we, Jimmy—you and I—are part of an integrated information-action unit."

Jimmy didn't have a clue what that meant, but Dr. Higgins sounded very excited about it. The doctor continued, "This means, Jimmy, that not only do we find out information, but we act on it—whatever it takes. It's called Black Ops, and that's where you come in."

While Dr. Higgins grew agitated talking to Jimmy, Paduk strolled round the room, looking quite bored. Dr. Higgins paid him no attention.

"You don't realize who you are, or what you are. But I do. I know everything about you, Jimmy. I know you down to the very last detail—details so small that you wouldn't even think they existed. I know you better than I know myself." Dr. Higgins was barely able to control his excitement. Then he said something that Jimmy didn't think he could possibly have heard correctly: "I designed you." The doctor's face contorted into a grin that tripled the number of lines on his face. Brown and yellow teeth bustled for position in his mouth.

Jimmy cast a glance at Paduk. The tall, broad officer was impassive.

"I'm sorry; what did you say?" Jimmy asked.

"I said that I designed you."

Jimmy didn't know what to do. Obviously this shriveled old man was crazy. But what about everyone else in the room, who was carrying on as if it were a normal day at work? Were they crazy too?

"If you look hard enough at yourself, Jimmy, if you close your eyes and look into yourself, you'll see that you already know it's true. I designed you, and a team of the finest genetic engineers in the world helped me build you. Almost all of them are dead now, though. I'm virtually the only one of the original team left." His voice had dropped, and the crack of emotion colored his words. "You are the future of military technology, young man."

Jimmy couldn't help but laugh. It was the only reasonable response. This had to be a joke. Dr. Higgins didn't respond. He just waited. He fixed his eyes on Jimmy's face and watched until the laughter faded away. Suddenly it wasn't funny anymore. Jimmy looked down at his shoes, the only things he was wearing that weren't Felix's, apart from his underwear.

He became aware of a grayness emerging inside his head, like a dim memory coming into focus. Something about what Dr. Higgins had said made too much sense for it to be untrue. It was as if Jimmy was being told something he had already known, but that he had forgotten many years ago.

Dr. Higgins saw the boy's face fall. "Jimmy, don't be scared. Don't worry. You are a remarkable thing." Jimmy didn't like being called a "thing," but he didn't interrupt. "You were designed to grow organically, as if you were a normal child. You were fabricated using chemical means, then hidden in a location known only to NJ7 and agents of NJ7, like your parents."

"My parents?"

"Of course."

Jimmy's heart twisted in his chest. "Are they here?"

Dr. Higgins caught Paduk's eye and gave a casual nod. Was that a nod to Jimmy? What did that mean? Did that mean his parents *were* there? Or was he just avoiding the question and telling Paduk to do something?

Paduk marched in his muscular fashion out of the room, back down the corridor they had come in by. It seemed like an eternity passed, and then his boots clicked back through the dark tunnel. Three figures moved into the light of the room: Paduk, followed by Jimmy's parents.

"Mum! Dad!" Jimmy ran over to them and pelted his mother with a hug. She squeezed back. "I missed you. What happened to you?"

"We missed you too, Jimmy."

"Dad, what happened?" Jimmy asked, extending the hug to his father.

"Kasimit will explain everything, Jimmy. You should listen to him."

Jimmy's beaming smile faded a little as he stood back. His parents . . . different. They were less soft, crisper, colder. He looked at them closely. His mother looked well, but Jimmy had never seen her dressed so smartly. She was wearing a sharp black business suit with a white shirt underneath, and her usually flowing hair was tied back efficiently.

Ian Coates looked even more alien. Jimmy's father stood up tall, with his shoulders pinned back. He was wearing the same kind of uniform as Paduk: light blue, with gold material dripping off every corner. It was less bright than Paduk's—faded with age perhaps—and on the breast there was a shorter row of medals. One thing stood out to Jimmy. He had noticed it on Paduk, but never expected to see it on his father. At the end of the row of medals was a thin, vertical line of material: a green stripe.

Before Dr. Higgins could continue his explanation, Jimmy blurted out the question that had been eating away at him: "Listen, Mr. Higgins—I mean, Dr. Higgins—he said that you were NJ7 agents. What does that mean?"

Ian and Helen Coates looked at each other. Dr. Higgins cleared his throat and spoke again. "I think it might be easier if I explain."

"Go ahead, Kasimit," said Jimmy's father.

"This is going to be difficult for you, Jimmy. You were not meant to know this until the age of eighteen, but the situation demands that I tell you now. Your parents aren't really your parents."

Is that it? Jimmy said to himself. If that was all, it would be a relief after everything he'd been through.

"So I'm adopted, right?" he said bluntly. "That's fine. Is this all just a fancy way of telling me I'm adopted?" Kasimit Higgins chuckled, but Jimmy's parents looked uneasy.

"No, no," Dr. Higgins said, "nothing like that." His eyes sparkled with intense delight. "You're state property."

"What?"

"I told you already: you weren't born. I designed you, and a team of experts like me built you."

"And what was I designed to do?" Jimmy whispered, terrified the answer was going to be worse than anything that had come before.

"Jimmy, you are an assassin," said Dr. Higgins with majesty.

"I . . . kill people?" The words struggled through his throat.

"Yes, and we're all very proud of you."

Jimmy couldn't breathe. He felt like his brain had been seized in a fist. He looked across the faces of the people lined up in front of him: Dr. Higgins, Paduk, his parents. Blank faces, all of them. Jimmy was aware that for the first time everyone else in the room had stopped typing and had turned to stare at him.

"How many people have I killed?" Jimmy had turned white, and his voice was thin. His mother put her hand to her mouth.

"Oh, Jimmy," she whispered, trembling slightly.

Dr. Higgins was far more robust. "Don't worry, Jimmy. You haven't killed a soul. Not yet. You're actually not meant to undertake a single mission until you're eighteen. That's when your training is technically complete." He tapped his pen against his chin and swiveled in his chair. "It seems, though, that some of your more basic skills have already developed, probably because your programming was responding to a perceived danger."

"What do you mean, my training? I've never been trained."

"Oh, but you have, Jimmy. To a very high level, and in a very sophisticated manner."

"I don't believe any of this." Jimmy shook his head. "It's all lies, isn't it? Why are you lying to me?"

"Ever have nightmares, Jimmy?" Dr. Higgins spoke quickly

and intensely, pointing his pen at Jimmy. "Bad dreams that you can't quite remember? Ever wake up in the morning feeling like you haven't really been to sleep?" Jimmy stared. "Marvelous. It's working a treat."

"What's working?"

"That's your training, Jimmy, your programming coming to life. It's *you* coming to life! You see, you don't really sleep, not in the human sense anyway." He was going to carry on, but Jimmy couldn't let this throwaway comment pass. He was getting angrier and angrier at the depth of the mystery that surrounded him.

"I am human. I'm just a normal kid. And I want to know why you've all been chasing me, and why you kidnapped my parents. Just let us go!"

"Jimmy." Dr. Higgins raised his voice to match Jimmy's. "You are thirty-eight percent human." The words bounced around the corridors. He banged his fist on the desk. "You are thirty-eight percent human! You are far from a 'normal kid,' whatever that may be, and we have been chasing you because we need you on a mission—right now."

His face had turned purple from shouting. He took two deep breaths to calm down, then carried on. "Your programming, a superadvanced system that is inside your head, develops slowly. And on your eighteenth birthday you would have come here voluntarily, to NJ7 headquarters, and reported for duty. When we came for you, the most basic part of your training kicked in—to evade capture at all costs. You would be more dangerous than ever if you fell into enemy hands."

Jimmy was stunned. He ran a thumb over the gash on his wrist. It was a reminder of everything about him that wasn't normal. Could it be true? Was he only 38 percent human? He felt normal, but then, of course he did. Everyone thinks that the way they feel is normal, but it's only normal to *them*.

Dr. Higgins started again, but more softly this time. "Your hair is getting long, Jimmy. You're supposed to keep it short."

Jimmy lifted his hand to his hair, dirty with the sweat of his nervousness. His mother answered for him. "There's a lot of things he's supposed to do but doesn't."

Dr. Higgins turned round in surprise. "What else?"

"Well, for a start, he doesn't like Chinese food."

"Doesn't like Chinese food?" He was shocked. "Is this true, Jimmy?"

Jimmy looked from Dr. Higgins to his mother and back, unsure about how to answer. "It kind of all tastes the same," he mumbled.

"Rubbish!" Dr. Higgins sprang out of his chair, suddenly more alive than ever. He started pacing the room. "Given the choice, an NJ7 agent will always choose food that comes with a weapon. Steaks are good—they come with steak knives, but chopsticks are just as lethal."

"That's ridiculous." Jimmy couldn't stop himself. Of all the things he had heard so far, that was the most outrageous.

"It might sound ridiculous to you, Jimmy, but chopsticks could save your life."

Jimmy imagined holding up a pair of chopsticks to defend himself. It was a stupid idea. He couldn't even eat with them without dropping noodles in his lap. His father stood as solid as a cliff face, unmoving, unmoved, but Jimmy could see his eyes flickering with emotion. Then Jimmy's mother motioned to him.

"Come here, Jimmy," she said, and bent down to hug him again. This time he was pulled so close he feared for his ribs. "Why are you doing this?" she barked at Dr. Higgins. "Can't you admit you failed? Look at him—he's human. And he could never kill anybody."

"His achievements in the last few days prove you wrong," Dr. Higgins said sternly. "He is thirty-eight percent human and he will kill. Pretty soon nobody else will be able to stop him."

Jimmy wriggled loose from his mother and protested. "I'm not killing anyone. It's wrong, and I don't know how."

"Don't be silly, Jimmy," said the doctor, bristling under his white coat. "Did you know how to run so fast? Did you know how to fly a helicopter? Did you know how to breath under-water?" Jimmy was taken aback. "Yes, we know everything you've been up to. Mrs. Doren is a loyal subject of the government. She told us everything you told her." Jimmy suddenly remembered Eva's mother bringing him more orange juice. She'd drugged him. "Listen, Jimmy, why do you think you jumped off the helicopter at Westminster Bridge? You had an instinct to come here, Jimmy—that's where we are right now! We're sitting under the Thames. You wanted to come to us, but didn't know why because you're not fully developed yet."

Jimmy thought back. With dangerous accuracy, things were starting to fit together. He *had* seen a green stripe in the water. It must have been indicating the entrance to this subterranean headquarters.

Dr. Higgins straightened his collar and dropped his pen down onto the desk.

"Don't be upset—it's a truly marvelous thing. You know so much that you don't realize, Jimmy. You'll soon find out,

though. It'll come from inside you, like everything else. . . ."
Dr. Higgins tailed off, lost in a new thought. He shuffled over
to one of the computers. "I'd like to see whether one particular
experiment has worked."

With a couple of clicks, music started seeping out of unseen
speakers. It was beautiful music, with a piano and a violin and
something that sounded to Jimmy like an accordion. In this
bleak surrounding it was totally out of place, but perhaps
because of the harsh environment, it seemed like the loveliest
music Jimmy had ever heard.

"This is tango music, Jimmy," hissed the doctor, overexcited. "Why not dance with your mother?"

"No way," said Jimmy. At the back of the room someone
else had slipped in, unnoticed. Only now did she speak. "How
about dancing with me, Jimmy?"

It was a familiar voice, and it chilled Jimmy's heart.

A LESSON IN FOOTWEAR

Jimmy was flabbergasted. The tango music washed around the room, and tapping her foot gently to the rhythm was Miss Bennett. He felt like he'd been kicked in the mouth by a rhino. She walked around to Jimmy's side of the desk and leaned back on it. There was a cheeky glint in her eye; her hair and makeup were far too glamorous for the surroundings. What was she doing here?

Her foot carried on tapping gently on the floor. That was it—her shoes. Jimmy's world disintegrated. Everything was numb. It was hard enough hearing that his father didn't make bottle tops, that both his parents were involved with this "NJ7" organization. Then he was told he was only 38 percent human. That still hadn't sunk in, and he still didn't actually believe it. But now, to cap it all, his teacher had sashayed into the secret headquarters wearing *those* shoes.

Jimmy stared at them. He'd seen that pattern before—worn by the third person who had come for him that night at his house. He had only seen the feet from under the car in the drive, and he had assumed they belonged to a man. But here they were again, and Miss Bennett's legs were definitely female.

"Surprised to see me, Jimmy?"

"Does this mean I get extra days off school?" He was trying to stay calm. He didn't want his teacher to know she had him ruffled.

"We'll see about that. First, I want to see what you can do." She stepped over and took Jimmy's left hand in her right, and put his right hand round her waist. "Dance," she ordered, as if she were setting extra homework.

Jimmy was mortified. He closed his eyes and put one foot clumsily forward, with no idea what he was doing. He thought he was going to step on Miss Bennett's foot, but to his astonishment, he felt himself gliding over the floor. Something had taken control of him.

He opened his eyes and saw himself guiding his teacher around the desk with grace and precision. The bold and delicate steps of the tango oozed out of him, like dancing a poem. He was brilliant. He just wished dancing with his teacher wasn't so . . . embarrassing. The tune came to an end, and Jimmy dipped Miss Bennett back for a showy finish. In the silence that followed the music, Jimmy froze, suddenly feeling ridiculous again.

Dr. Higgins broke into applause. "Apparently it is no longer necessary for an assassin to blend in at embassy functions, Jimmy. But I couldn't pass up the opportunity to endow you with skills more interesting than murder. You have surpassed all my expectations."

Miss Bennett pulled herself out of Jimmy's hold and straightened her suit, flicking the hair out of her face. "If you can kill as well as you dance," she said, "God help our enemies."

"I c-came to you for help," stuttered Jimmy.

"How do you think you found my address so easily? A box with 'Staff Addresses' written on it? My, how convenient."

"You left it on the desk for us to find? You planted it? Why didn't you just come and get me from Felix's house?"

"That's what we did. Didn't you notice? But it took time to authorize use of Code Three weaponry." Jimmy wanted to ask what that meant, but Paduk cut in.

"Miss Bennett," he said, cracking his jaw, "hadn't we better get things started?"

"Yes, Paduk, thank you." She waved a desultory hand in his direction. "If all we did was dance all day, this country would disintegrate into chaos. Or worse, it would become France. Come on, Jimmy." She turned briskly to the exit, her hair swishing behind her, but Jimmy didn't follow.

"What about Mum and Dad?" he said. His mother crossed the room to put her arm round him.

"Jimmy," answered Miss Bennett, "your parents will be fine as long as you do everything I tell you to do. We are all on the same side." Seeing that he was unconvinced, she carried on. "The secrecy has been necessary, Jimmy, for everyone's survival—including your own—and the good of the nation. Well, don't just stand around like lemons; explain it to him." Jimmy was shocked to see that she was addressing his parents—and they were accepting it.

"Jimmy," started his father, "I am sorry we haven't been

honest with you. I don't make bottle tops. Before you were born, your mother and I were agents working for the government, first for MI6, then thirteen years ago we were transferred to the newly set-up agency: NJ7." He hesitated, so Helen Coates picked up the story.

"We were selected for a very special mission. It was a great honor. And it still is. It's you." Jimmy was trying to picture his mother and father working together before he was born, with Georgie as a baby. He didn't want to imagine what terrible things they had done. He looked into his mother's eyes and wanted to reach out when he saw them filling with moisture, but Miss Bennett interrupted without any sympathy.

"It *was* a great honor. You are the first of your kind. The first one we can use, anyway." She threw a glance at Dr. Higgins as she said this, and he seemed to shrink for a second in her accusatory gaze. "You were meant to become operational at eighteen, but we need you now. Your entire upbringing has been carefully planned and overseen by NJ7 agents, some of whom even your parents didn't know about."

Jimmy's father snapped his head round. "What?"

"Did you think we were going to trust you two alone with a thirty-million-pound weapon?"

"But you were there, and Dr. Higgins of course—who else was necessary?" Ian Coates was indignant at the implications, but Miss Bennett just laughed.

"What about the seventeen different agents who have acted characters called the Bournes over the last eleven years? You lived next door and you never bothered to meet them. I'm sorry to say there may be more parent in you than agent."

The Bournes—Jimmy knew that name. When Paduk had

been pretending to be Sergeant Atkinson, he had claimed that the Bournes had called the police. The more he discovered, the less he liked. Everything had been determined for him years ago—before he was born. There had been no choice for him in anything.

"Now Jimmy"—Miss Bennett turned back to him—"NJ7 will look after your parents, and you will come with me." She beckoned him with a finger. Paduk stood close behind him, breathing onto the top of Jimmy's head. There was nothing for it but to move.

"But," Helen Coates started, "you said we could—"

"The plan has changed," Miss Bennett interrupted. "Let the boy do his job, then you'll be free to see him again—between missions, that is. If the boy doesn't do his job, on the other hand, you will both be dead."

Jimmy's head snapped round, his mind spinning. Suddenly the light in the room seemed too bright.

"You can't threaten us, Miss Bennett," said Ian Coates, keeping his eyes on Paduk. "Do I have to point out that we are more senior than you?"

"Ha! You've been out of the loop too long, Ian. You'll all do exactly what I say. Kasimit, Jimmy, come with me." She marched out down the corridor without a backward glance. Dr. Higgins scurried after her, waving to Jimmy to come with him. But Jimmy didn't move.

Paduk looked between Ian and Helen Coates. "Off you go, son," he said. "I'm looking after your parents now."

Jimmy was furious. He threw himself at Paduk, but the giant man was quick to hop out of the way.

"Jimmy, stop that!" shouted his father. "You'll complete

your mission! We'll be fine. It's for the good of the nation."

Then Jimmy heard his mother's voice raised in anger: "Ian! How could you? He's our son."

"No—he's our job."

Jimmy looked from one to the other, then at the rocky face of Paduk. He didn't know what to do with his anger anymore. It was confused now, and it stifled his breathing.

"Jimmy, you don't have to do this," said his mother softly, but his father's face said the opposite.

Jimmy listened to the footsteps of Miss Bennett and Dr. Higgins clipping away through the hallways.

"You lied to me," he whispered, and ran after them.

Jimmy's training took place in a room as bare as it could be, except for two facing chairs. It was his training room, class-room, and bedroom. His only visitors were Dr. Higgins, Paduk, and Miss Bennett. He washed in a bathroom down the hallway, and food was brought to him at all the right times. He slept on the floor. Worse than being confined, though, was the time alone to reflect. His mind seemed to take distorted pleasure in replaying those moments over and over: first, the terror that Miss Bennett would kill his family, then the anger at his parents for lying to him all these years. During the day, his jaw was clenched, his fists tight. When he slept, his nightmares were more intense, more powerful, but just as hard to remember.

Every morning was spent with Dr. Higgins.

"Let your instincts take control," he announced when he strode into the training room. The old man grew more and more mobile as time went on, as if getting younger himself through the excitement of training the boy he had designed.

"Abandon your conscious thoughts and leave yourself behind."

At first it was impossible. Jimmy's brain held on tight to the picture of his mother's face as she said, "You don't have to do this." Another lie. Of course he had to. How could his parents have been so stupid as to get themselves into this situation? He could only stop that thought by deliberately worrying about Georgie, or wondering what had happened to Felix. But after four days, Jimmy was finally able to stifle his thoughts long enough for his programming to take control. On the fifth morning, Dr. Higgins took matters to the next level.

"You kill with a single blow to the neck," he said, chopping his hand down gleefully. "At the back, or at the nerve cluster in the base of the throat."

It sounded so sick and clinical to Jimmy. It was an exact prescription: a tablespoon of oil, a handful of walnuts, and a single blow to the neck. Death's recipe. Jimmy wanted to shudder, but put aside his human reactions and let his mind go its own way, just as he had been told.

"Is that clear, Jimmy? A single blow to the neck?" Dr. Higgins peered at him through the creases where his eyes hid. "I don't have to teach you how to do it, because you already know. There are also some more inventive ways of killing in there, but strictly for your own amusement and education. They may not develop for a couple of years, but you should be aware of their existence."

"In where?"

"Where, boy? In your head, of course! So switch it on!" Jimmy wasn't sure whether Dr. Higgins actually meant him to literally find a switch and turn his head on, but he guessed it was just a figure of speech telling him to listen harder or something. He was used to those.

From then on, Dr. Higgins kept on telling him that he already knew how to do everything if he checked his own instincts. What was the point of all this training if he knew it all anyway? Jimmy wondered. But he could tell they were paranoid that something would go wrong because he was still only eleven. The killer they wanted should be eighteen.

In the afternoons, Jimmy was allowed to leave his room, accompanied by Paduk, to run round the streets of Westminster. It was almost a pleasure. Jogging through St. James's Park was the only time Jimmy could clear his mind of NJ7 and thoughts of killing. Paduk rarely said a word, just keeping pace, pounding onward. They shared only one real conversation. It came on their fourth outing together.

"Why do I have to run?" asked Jimmy. "I thought I was automatically fit."

"I'm running for fitness," answered Paduk. "You're running for the fresh air." Sweat matted Paduk's hair and streamed down his clifflike cheeks. Jimmy wasn't even out of breath.

Suddenly Paduk held out his arm and stopped him. "You're going to do this right, aren't you?" Paduk knelt down and looked intensely into Jimmy's eyes, gripping his shoulders. Jimmy looked away. "Tell me that you're going to do this right."

"Do what?" Jimmy could see the genuine concern behind the iron of Paduk's face.

"Your mission."

"I don't even know what my mission is yet. Do *you* know?"

Paduk laughed softly, although he wasn't smiling. He was searching Jimmy's face for something, some reaction that

Jimmy didn't know he had to give. It was as if Paduk were trying to distinguish the human from the machine. Then, standing up, he looked out across the park at something behind the ornate foliage.

"Do you know who lives there, Jimmy?" Jimmy followed Paduk's gaze to the glowing cream splendor of Buckingham Palace. "I love my country, Jimmy, and Britain needs people like us to protect her. You and me, that's what we do. We protect our country." Jimmy was a little unsettled by Paduk's passionate speech; he just wanted to start running again. "It's for the good of the country, Jimmy, so please—do it right."

Paduk stood slowly and clicked his jaw, then set off. Jimmy was too taken aback for a moment to follow, then quickly had to catch up. They didn't talk again.

"Come with me, Jimmy," cooed Miss Bennett, strutting in to curtail another passionate speech from Dr. Higgins. She swung her hips as she whisked Jimmy through the stark passages at a domineering pace. Jimmy struggled to remind himself that this woman had once been his teacher; now she'd taken control over every aspect of his life.

Eventually they came to a small silver door. Miss Bennett pushed it open and waved Jimmy past her. He emerged in the back room of a shop—a tailor's fitting room, with mirrors on all four walls and rolls of material stacked up to the ceiling. Jimmy could hear traffic. Back in the real world, he thought. Somehow they must have woven their way to street level.

Miss Bennett let the door swing shut between her and Jimmy. On his side it looked like another mirror. Reflected four times was a small man, with half-moon glasses perched on top of his head and a tape measure garlanded round his neck. Jimmy didn't need specially programmed instincts to tell him that this was a tailor.

In no time, he had a completely new outfit. He gleamed in a smart black shirt that caught the light with its sheen. It felt a little too much like a girly silk shirt to Jimmy. At least the trousers were comfortable, and the sneakers looked pretty cool—again, all black. The breast pocket boasted the only dash of color: a green stripe. Then he was shunted back through the mirror door, where Miss Bennett was waiting.

"I was expecting a suit," he announced as soon as he saw her.

"I was expecting a raise, but what can you do?" She marched off through the corridors again, leaving Jimmy to follow.

"Do I get gadgets now?" he called after her.

"Jimmy, you *are* a gadget: sixty-two percent of you is earth's finest technological hardware."

"The rest of me was expecting a gadget or two."

"You'll learn." They were making headway through the gray bricks again.

"Not even exploding chewing gum?" Jimmy asked.

"Not even spearmint chewing gum."

They stopped outside another of NJ7's rare doors. It was just the same as the others: no door handle, plain metal, except for one detail. Three-quarters of the way up were painted two black numerals: a one and a zero.

"Where are the other nine doors?" Jimmy asked, boldly.

"There are hardly any doors at NJ7 HQ," replied Miss Bennett in her velvet voice. "It's for security." That sounded backward to Jimmy, but Miss Bennett continued, "If we ever need to, we can flood the whole complex in just two minutes. One hundred and twenty seconds, and nothing would be left breathing. Except you, of course."

Before Jimmy could respond, Miss Bennett pushed the door firmly and guided Jimmy through it. Just as he realized she wasn't following him, the door slammed shut.

"Jimmy Coates, I have been waiting for the pleasure of this day for twenty years."

The prime minister towered over him—much taller than he seemed on television. He looked older as well, more frail, but it was unmistakably Ares Hollingdale. The thin gray hair softened the corners of his head, and the wrinkles in his face all seemed to point toward the end of his nose, which reached out a little too inquisitively. There were heavy gray bags under his eyes.

"Welcome to Number Ten, Downing Street, Jimmy. Can I offer you tea?"

ONCOMING TRAIN

The reception room of Number Ten was perfect and seemed a million miles from the den of NJ7. The carpet was thick, the ceilings tall, and cruel portraits of cruel people covered the walls. Beneath the paintings stood a host of people who almost resembled the images: secretaries, assistants, security guards. With silent organization that could have been a dance routine, Jimmy had been escorted in, served tea and cookies, and made to feel like a dignitary. Now he sat swamped in a too-soft armchair. The level of the armrests was almost above his head, and the tea was placed on a table just out of reach. He decided to let it cool and made occasional dives for the cookies instead.

"I am Ares Hollingdale," began the PM as if announcing the start of a play.

"I know," said Jimmy, and then as an afterthought he added, "I'm Jimmy," even though he had already been addressed by name. Once again Jimmy's head teemed with questions. What had the prime minister meant when he said he had been waiting for twenty years for this moment? Had all this been planned since before Jimmy was even born? If *born* was the right word—Dr. Higgins would say *built*.

After the pleasantries, everyone in the room was waved away by the prime minister, and the two of them were left alone, except for the painted faces staring down from the walls.

Hollingdale reached for the teapot.

"Do you know what I am doing, Jimmy?"

"Pouring yourself another cup of tea?"

"I mean for the country." His voice was definitely that of an old man. It was deep and throaty, drawn out from years of speaking in Parliament.

"Oh, I see. No, I don't know what you're doing for the country."

"I am making it great." The PM's eyes fired up as he spoke, and the veins on his neck stood to purple attention. "Gone are the days when any fool in the street could have his say in how to run a country. Tell me, Jimmy, if you wanted to build a ship, would you ask a hundred random people, or would you go to an expert shipbuilder?"

"You're building a ship?" Jimmy was more confused than ever.

"No, no, no! It's an example, child. If I *were* building a ship, I would employ an expert. Now, it's the same with running a country. Why should we ask every single person his opinion, when we can ask experts?"

"Experts in running countries?"

"Exactly! That's the spirit!" Ares Hollingdale rattled his teacup with excitement. Jimmy was growing less comfortable with this man by the second. He wished the PM had stayed safely behind a TV screen. "So I don't need to ask the fools and the simpletons; I don't need the man in the street telling me what to do. I am building a stronger country for all of us."

"Great." Jimmy was trying his hardest to avoid Hollingdale's eyes, which were almost throbbing in his skull. Then the PM grew suddenly reflective, and sat back in his armchair.

"I remember the day when I thought something like you would never be necessary. You were never meant for the sort of job you're going on, Jimmy."

Just get to the point, Jimmy was thinking—what job is it?

"You were a special project. And you were going to protect us from the nation's foreign enemies."

The prime minister closed his eyes and let the room absorb the silence. For a second, Jimmy wondered if he had fallen asleep, or even died, but then he sprang back to life, with even more vigor. "Now we need to call on you to resist the enemies within our great nation! The naysayers, the traitors, the old-fashioned democrats who stick up for the fools." He spat out his words, full of venom, and they sprayed over the cookies. Jimmy made a mental note not to eat any more.

"Sir," he said meekly, keen to get away from this frightening man as soon as he could, "apparently I am an assassin. But I don't know what my job is yet—"

"Your mission!"

"Yes, my mission."

"We are all very proud of you, Jimmy, and of what you are going to do. The Green Stripe has found another worthy instrument, I can tell straightaway. I like you. You are NJ7 through and through."

Jimmy cringed. Praise from this man didn't feel like praise

from anybody else. It felt like a stomachache.

"Now I think it's time," the prime minister continued. "The first mission for the new generation of NJ7 agents. When you leave here, Miss Bennett will brief you. I assure you, she's worth your rapt attention. Together, we can make this country stronger, Jimmy, and bigger."

Bigger? How could you make a country bigger? Jimmy was about to ask, but the prime minister hadn't finished. His eyes roamed over Jimmy's face, and he spoke with an unhurried menace.

"Has the importance of your mission been made clear to you, young man?"

"Y-yes," Jimmy stuttered. "It's to protect the country."

"Ah, no, I meant the importance to *you*—personally." The corners of the prime minister's mouth curled upward minutely. "And the importance to your family."

His meaning was clear just from the threatening glee in his eyes. Jimmy's throat snapped tight, and time seemed to stop. He understood perfectly. By the time he had pulled himself back to the present, the prime minister was already out of the room, replaced by some of his entourage. The meeting was over. Jimmy was escorted back through the metal door.

The target's face was familiar—Jimmy had seen it on television that last night at home. Christopher Viggo. A thorn in Hollingdale's side. When Viggo got the chance, he spoke passionately in public, campaigning for old freedoms—"out-of-date freedoms" Miss Bennett called them. He kept popping up to ask the prime minister awkward questions in front of the press. But Viggo was becoming more than just an embarrassment. Miss Bennett said that he was dangerous now that he had started gathering support, threatening to put together an opposition. There hadn't been an opposition for years. What was the point when you couldn't vote for it?

So Christopher Viggo had to go. But to have someone kill him in public would be a disaster—everyone would suspect the government, and it would make the man more popular than ever. You can't murder a young, good-looking dissident and expect his memory to disappear. But he was a hard man to reach in private. The plan was to do it up close, so no one would suspect anything except bad luck.

Viggo's features were soon impressed on Jimmy's retinas. But now Jimmy was standing on the corner of Downing Street watching the flesh-and-blood target swagger away in the drizzle from his "specially arranged debate" with the prime minister. Such an obvious trap. Why couldn't Viggo have stayed at home? They had lured him to this special meeting through an ad in the papers, and now it was up to Jimmy to follow him. When they were far enough from the prime minister to allay suspicion, Jimmy was to kill him, then report back. Simple. If anybody got in his way, he was to kill them too.

Jimmy peered at him through the rain. Viggo was younger and better-looking than the prime minister, and, according to Miss Bennett, even more charismatic. No wonder Hollingdale wanted him dead. His soft brown eyes glinted above sharp cheekbones, stubbled in a way that reminded Jimmy more of a pop star than a politician. Poor man. He was going to be dead pretty soon and had no idea. The fact that Jimmy was going to be the one to kill him was nasty—horrific even.

Jimmy had never wanted to kill anybody. Sure, there had

been people at school he'd wished would just disappear, but to kill them was something different. It made him feel sick. How could anybody do it? And how could anybody sit in his comfortable armchair with tea and cookies, and calmly send someone to do something so vile? That's when Jimmy started to understand why they needed someone who was almost a robot: 38 percent human. Only 38 percent of him would have twinges of remorse about killing. The rest was programmed to destroy, regardless of right and wrong. The blood drained from his face.

All he wanted to do was run away. Nobody was watching him. It was the first time in ages that he hadn't been accompanied by someone from NJ7—his was a solo mission. But Jimmy knew he couldn't—it would mean abandoning his parents. Even though he hadn't forgiven them for lying to him, there was no question of leaving them to die. Jimmy wished that he wasn't human at all. Maybe it would have stifled the cries of his conscience.

But Jimmy's human part was terrified at the truth that was slowly sinking in. He was a killer. He was evil. At times he thought he could feel murder dripping off his skin. It was always there, just under his senses. Designed and built as a killer, it was just a matter of time before he did someone harm.

He tried to shake off his morbid thoughts. It's just like homework, he told himself. He had always suspected homework would be the death of someone.

Jimmy wiped the rain off the side of his face with his sleeve. The special Green Stripe shirt was remarkable. He didn't need a coat because it was so warm, and the rain just flicked off it. It wasn't even wet when you touched it. He trailed Viggo through the streets of central London, through the crowds of the gray afternoon. It was no trouble at all staying unnoticed, and there were enough people about for Jimmy to be able to follow quite close.

Viggo had his coat pulled up round his ears and walked briskly, wanting to get out of the rain. Around him, umbrellas jostled for position, then floated past. Jimmy wove a path through the raincoats and puddles, always keeping his eye on the back of Viggo's head. Viggo didn't glance back once. He couldn't have suspected he was being followed. If he'd been expecting danger, he would have had bodyguards, Jimmy thought. Maybe he had a higher opinion of the PM than he should have had. Or maybe he was armed.

They came to Embankment subway station. Viggo's hand snapped the ticket from his pocket and threaded it into the machine. Jimmy was prepared for this. The one piece of equipment he had been allowed was a subway ticket. He passed through the same machine at a safe distance.

The station was busy and had that familiar dank smell that the subway grows when it rains—like a stray dog. The underground tunnels reminded Jimmy of NJ7 headquarters, and he wondered whether the two systems ever linked up. It wouldn't have surprised him. If they had a secret door into a tailor's shop, and another one right into the prime minister's residence, who knew where else they had access to? People bustled everywhere, through the ticket hall, on the escalators, the stairs. It was getting harder to keep an eye on Viggo, especially as Jimmy was shorter than everyone who came between them. He was fairly sure he still had him, though. The upturned collar, the hunched shoulders.

Jimmy fixed his gaze on the back of the man's coat as he came to a halt on the Northern Line platform. Two minutes to the next train. Jimmy wiped his nose on his sleeve. His hair was dripping wet from the rain, but he was sweating too. Then he felt a strange heat building inside him. It was coming. The machine part of him was taking over again. Why now?

The dark power accumulated, swirling round his insides. As it swooped up the side of his neck and over his head, Jimmy realized that this was it. The perfect time to kill. The perfect place for an "accident." He wanted to stop himself, but couldn't push the urge down. It was buzzing through him— familiar, yet . . . different. He had never felt the power of his killing instinct before. Jimmy tried to open his mouth to scream, but he had no control anymore. His body was succumbing to his programming.

As if from a distant viewpoint, but trapped inside his own head, he watched his hands starting to move. He felt his weight move forward. "Take control, take control!" he said to himself, but the rest of him wasn't listening. "Take control, control!" It was all he could do. Now that the moment had come, he wanted more than anything to stop it. Going through the training, he had been able to ignore the truth that he was going to end a man's life, but here it was. The time had come so soon.

Jimmy crept toward the edge of the platform, right up to his target. One push at the right moment, and that would be it. Simple. The machine had taken over. The weak child was only able to watch. He edged closer, elbowing commuters out of the way, until he stood right behind the dripping coat that entombed his victim. The next train was due. Dust blew around his feet. The wind from the tunnel picked up, hot and filthy. The tracks crackled.

Jimmy was breathing calmly, but inside he was panicking. His heartbeat was steady—taken over by the unfeeling killer while the human Jimmy was pleading silently inside. The noise mounted. The lights of the fatal train blinked into view round the bend of the tunnel. Jimmy's hands wavered over his pockets, like a gunslinger waiting to draw. The man in front of him suspected nothing as he turned to watch the train approach.

In a flash, Jimmy's body twisted. He leaned into the man and pretended to stumble. With the weight of his shoulder and the guidance of his palms, Jimmy shoved the man forward into the path of the train. He turned away as the poor fool let out a yelp of shock. Jimmy started moving toward the exit, but someone blocked his path—Christopher Viggo. Jimmy had pushed the wrong man.

The tall, chiseled figure of Viggo was moving toward the tracks. He had seen the other man falling. Did he see Jimmy push him? The train was still hurtling forward, the man still falling into the pit that would mean his death. But Viggo was there, jumping into the path of the train himself. The driver's face was a picture of terror. The brakes screeched like the screams of a thousand murder victims. The man Jimmy had pushed was still flailing in the air when Viggo lunged under him, straining every muscle. He just managed to avoid the tracks with his feet, which would have meant electrocution, and caught the man round his middle.

As soon as Viggo landed, he jumped back up again, but he wasn't quick enough. The train was surely going to hit them both. Christopher Viggo desperately flung his legs out to the side, toward the front of the train. His feet smacked into the driver's window, and he was thrown off the front of the train back onto the platform. The commuters pulled back in fright as Viggo pounced on them, clutching the man he had just saved. Together they rolled across the dust of the platform. The train rattled past, coming to a stop just where it always did, and the doors slid open as if nothing had happened. The driver must have thought he imagined the whole thing—or didn't want to try describing it to his seniors, anyway.

Jimmy was wheezing with the shock. How had he confused the two men? He felt like the idiot his sister was always telling him he was.

It took all Jimmy's mental determination to board the train after the fuss had died down. The air was hardly reaching his lungs. He wished he could just walk away, but it was his duty to finish the job—however badly he had started it. Jimmy wasn't thinking of his duty to his country, though. He was thinking of his duty to his family. It was that simple: take one life to save three others, as far as Jimmy was concerned.

On the train, Jimmy watched while Christopher Viggo was treated like a hero. Some people even recognized him and started asking him about all his political activity. Jimmy wasn't surprised that people warmed to him. He had just saved someone's life, after all. Jimmy picked up bits of the conversation and heard Viggo calling the prime minister things like "tyrant" and "dictator." Jimmy didn't care anymore. He just wanted to get out and go home.

But he had a reason to obey orders. He felt his love for his parents weeping inside him. Could love ever be a reason to kill?

130

Jimmy had never felt so terrible. The strange force subsided; his hands started shaking, and his mouth was parched. It took all his effort to stop himself from throwing up. This is no job for a child, he thought, even one who's only partially human.

The train gradually emptied as it moved up the Northern Line. By the time it emerged into the open air, there were plenty of seats free. Jimmy sat at one end of the carriage, while Viggo was still deep in conversation with one of his new fans at the other end. Jimmy felt conspicuous. He wished NJ7 had given him some sort of cover; even a school uniform and a bag full of books would have given him a reason to be on the train. As it was, he was getting strange looks from everyone. A kid on the subway dressed in black silk was pretty unusual.

At Finchley Central, Viggo rose and Jimmy followed. It had stopped raining now, but the late afternoon was still darker than it should have been for the time of year. This was a part of London Jimmy had never been to before, and it took on the eerie qualities of a nightmare. Viggo turned up his collar. A terrible day to die, thought Jimmy.

He stalked Viggo, staying back, but keeping the man in view. They walked along the bridge over the track, which spilled into a side street at the end, and Viggo turned up the hill toward the main road.

Jimmy paused. His head kept telling him he didn't have to go through with this, but he knew that wasn't true. His parents might be his supervising agents, but they were still his parents. He remembered his mother screaming at him to run when NJ7 had first come to get him. She didn't want this life for him. Maybe if he could finish this job properly, they would all be able to retire, and his dad would be able to *really* start making bottle tops.

Viggo's coat was swishing round the corner. No more indecision. This was it. Jimmy ran up the street after him.

There was very little traffic, but the few cars that there were drove too fast. They sprayed the rain on the surface of the road into the air. The gray mist circled round Viggo as he sprinted across the road. Jimmy waited with his back turned, watching the reflection in the window of another closed-down American burger chain. He saw Viggo glance casually over his shoulder. Did he know he was being followed?

Viggo took a fork off the main road, and then with one last glance back down the street, he disappeared into a doorway. Jimmy crossed the road and sat in a bus shelter, still watching out of the corner of his eye. His insides twitched. Jimmy Coates, killer, was getting ready to strike.

14

IZGARU

IZGARU—the golden letters curled out around one another, far too grand for the restaurant they adorned. The dark green wooden frontage was chipped and faded; the glass in the windows was filthy. Jimmy's focus shifted between the empty tables inside and the bedraggled boy reflected back at him from across the road. The menu posted by the door was barely legible because of the dirt that had built up on it. It was a Turkish place—hummus, kebabs, baklava. Jimmy was hungry. It was too early for anybody to be eating, so Izgaru was deserted.

Then he spotted activity inside. Viggo was moving between the ghostlike tables, with their white cloths hanging like shrouds. He sat down with his back to the window, pulled out a pen from his top pocket, and began working on some papers. He looked comfortable. Jimmy started thinking about how he was going to do the deed: a single blow to the neck.

Even as the thought was going through his mind, he felt disgusted. He wished the unfeeling, nonhuman part of him would take over and spare him the nausea. It was the real Jimmy, though, who nervously crossed the road, every step taking him nearer to his target.

When he came close, the door to the kitchen sprang open, and another man entered the restaurant, carrying a plate piled high with meat. His white apron was covered in grease, and his fat hands quivered with the heat of the food. Jimmy watched him return to the kitchen. Viggo had hardly acknowledged the arrival of his snack. It looked so tasty.

Jimmy realized he couldn't just walk in through the front door. There might be a bell or buzzer, which would immediately give him away. He ran round the side of the building, looking for a back entrance. There wasn't one, but there was an open window.

The curls of steam told him that it belonged to the kitchen. Jimmy jumped up and tried to grab the ledge. It was slippery from the rain and too thin to grasp. He tried again, but again he just fell back to the gutter. Much as he hated the thought of it, he needed to rouse the killer inside him.

He closed his eyes and clenched his stomach muscles. Come on, he thought, then he forced it out through gritted teeth: "Come *on*."

There it was—a faint swirling, as if a worm were wriggling its way through his gut. Gradually it grew, until it was a surging, twisting ball trying to burst out of his chest. Jimmy felt his posture change. His shoulders rose up, tightening. His legs moved slightly apart, and his knees flexed—ready for action. He had to retain control though. That was the hardest thing, but he knew he could do it. He had summoned this—definitely.

Now when he jumped, he sprang so high that he was able

to grab hold of the open window with both hands. With one fast tug, he ripped the whole thing out of the wall. As the wood casing came away, the faintest crumbling of the brick round the edge was the only noise. The glass was still intact.

The man in the kitchen looked out of the window that was no longer there, astonished. Then he saw two small hands clutching the wall from below. His hand edged across the countertop toward the handle of his biggest knife.

The kitchen was boiling hot. The stifling air hit Jimmy in the face as he dove through the hole. He landed with a forward roll, his hand resting for an instant on the work surface, where his fist closed around a small cabbage. The fat chef drew breath to shout, and the silver flash of the knife cut through the steam, but Jimmy was too fast. His foot slammed into the chef's hand, sending the knife hurtling into the wall. It stuck there, vibrating. Jimmy's other foot smashed into the man's chest, knocking all the wind out of him. The overblown cook collapsed backward. Jimmy stuffed the cabbage into the man's mouth, where it stoppered a scream before it began. When the chef's head hit the tiles, he was knocked out cold.

There had been barely a noise. Only the ping of the knife in the wall, and the heavy splat of an overweight man being knocked over.

Jimmy prowled toward the door to the restaurant. He moved like a shadow past the roasting carcasses, the piles of lettuce leaves, and the bowl of mints.

Christopher Viggo was still sitting at the same table, paperwork on one side, half a plate of food on the other. He raised his head when the door swung open.

"Yannick?" he said, but instead he saw a black-clad, eleven-year-old boy staring at him, sucking a mint. Viggo's face dropped. His eyes went straight to the green stripe on Jimmy's shirt.

"Mitchell, or James?" said Viggo, his voice rich and calm.

The question held Jimmy back. He tried not to let his confusion show. How did this man know his name? And who was Mitchell? There was no way this man could mean *that* Mitchell. . . .

"My name's Jimmy," he said. It was hard to speak with the surging waves of energy that swelled inside him.

"And you've come to kill me," announced Viggo with a reflective tilt of his head.

"It's for the good of the country," replied Jimmy.

Christopher Viggo slowly stood up, dropping his pen and raising his hands to show he wasn't armed. His chair creaked on the floor. Jimmy guarded the door.

"I knew they'd come for me eventually, but I thought they'd wait until you all grew up," said Viggo, edging ever so slowly round the table.

Jimmy didn't move, but watched his target edging sideways. A napkin hung from the top of Viggo's trousers, almost like a surrender flag. Viggo didn't look like he was going to give up, though. There was a glint in his eye.

"How do you like NJ7, Jimmy?"

"You know about NJ7?" Jimmy couldn't stop himself from asking. "You know *me*?" So much for the secrecy. Then the truth dawned on him, just as Viggo explained.

"I used to be like you—except I'm one hundred percent human. I used to wear the Green Stripe too." A strange smile tinged the corners of his mouth. Happy memories? Or happy they were over? Jimmy couldn't tell.

Suddenly there was a rush of doubt in Jimmy's mind. Why hadn't Miss Bennett mentioned that Christopher Viggo used to be an NJ7 agent? No wonder they needed Jimmy to do the job. No one else could get close.

The doubt must have flashed across Jimmy's face, because Viggo chose that moment. He rushed over to the restaurant's front door, his napkin floating to the floor. He was in great shape and he could run like a sprinter, but he didn't make it across the room. Jimmy bounded through the tables and into Viggo's path. Broken glasses scattered across the floor, and a table blocked the back door—there was no way out. Jimmy sprang toward Viggo, his insides raging with his mechanical instinct: kill.

Killing a former NJ7 agent wasn't a simple matter, though. Viggo was strong and quick. He turned to the side and leaned his shoulder forward. Jimmy hit it full on and bounced over the top of Viggo's back. He landed with a crash on the next table.

"Listen, Jimmy," said Viggo, as Jimmy brushed breadstick crumbs from his front, "why do you think I run my operation from a Turkish restaurant?"

Jimmy crouched, ready to pounce. "You should have chosen Chinese. At least with chopsticks you'd be able to defend yourself." With that, he launched another violent assault, this time flying feet first at Viggo's knees.

Viggo was expecting it. He easily skipped out of the way and kicked a chair into Jimmy's path. The boy clattered into it ungracefully.

"No, Jimmy," said Viggo, strolling back over to his table, "you're forgetting one thing."

"What's that?"

"Kebabs are served on skewers." With lightning hands

Viggo grabbed a used skewer from his plate. He threw himself onto the floor and rolled under the table next to Jimmy. Like a knockout punch, the skewer stabbed into the wall a millimeter from Jimmy's ear. It splintered a hair.

"You should cut your hair," said Viggo, pulling the weapon back. Jimmy kicked the man away with one powerful jab. He jumped up and danced across the tabletops back to the center of the room. There, he reached down and plucked up the other skewer from Viggo's half-eaten meal. This one still had meat on it.

Jimmy didn't even know that he could fence. But he could. It crept up on him, just like his karate, his jumping, his swimming, and all his talents. But Viggo had been trained by NJ7 too. They matched each other lunge for lunge, parry for parry. Jimmy was astonished at the speed of his own hands, one holding the skewer, the other extended behind him for balance. Bound by the sparks of metal that flew from their makeshift swords, Jimmy Coates and Christopher Viggo skipped round the restaurant, dodging the tables and each other's attacks. But Jimmy never stopped thinking.

He swung round, fending off a counterattack from Viggo, swapping the spike to his left hand. With his right, he jerked a tablecloth away from its table. The place setting crashed to the floor. Jimmy flung the white cloth into the air between them. The sheet flapped open, completely obscuring the duelers' views. Then Jimmy hopped up onto a chair and jumped at the cloth, feetfirst.

The full force of Jimmy's leap hit Viggo in the face. Viggo stumbled backward, but he steadied himself on the table behind him.

Jimmy had spun round to land safely on his front. He bit a

chunk of kebab meat off his skewer. He was hungry. It tasted like chicken.

Just then, the door to the kitchen swung open. Yannick. The chubby chef in the greasy apron. In one hand was a cabbage, in the other, a huge knife. He dropped the cabbage and rubbed his head, then joined the fray, leading with his blade. Now Jimmy was fighting both of them at once. Fortunately the chef was much slower, and obviously hadn't had the same training.

"Why don't you have a bodyguard, Viggo?" Jimmy said, clashing swords with one opponent and fending off the other's attacks with his kicks.

"Don't worry about me. I know how to handle myself," came the unruffled answer. "But I can't cook. So it's more useful to have a chef."

Jimmy ducked under the two daggers, then jumped into the air. He landed on the edge of a table at the other side of the room. At that moment, Viggo flung his spike at Jimmy. It whirred through the air, chicken fat still glistening on the metal. It was dead on target. Jimmy hit the edge of the table and the whole thing catapulted upward, where Viggo's weapon stuck harmlessly in the wood. Then Jimmy caught the table and hurled it across the room. It belted Yannick in the face. He crumpled and fell, knocked out for the second time that night.

Viggo was unarmed now. Jimmy saw his chance. He was at the mercy of his programming, buzzing with the thrill of its power—the strongest yet. Viggo was making for the kitchen door. Jimmy threw himself across the floorboards. He slid on his front, arms outstretched, still clutching his kebab stick. As he reached Viggo, he slammed the skewer into the ground and held on to it. His legs flew up into the air with the impetus of his jump, and his heels smacked Viggo in the back of the head. Jimmy came to rest flat on his back, his arms stretched out above his head, still holding the skewer.

Viggo was staggering but he wasn't down, even though the force of Jimmy's assault had been massive. He was reeling toward the door. One more step . . . but the world was spinning. His foot came down on Yannick's discarded cabbage. He slipped and hit the floor hard.

Jimmy tossed the now empty skewer over his shoulder and wiped his mouth with his sleeve. The juices of the kebab stirred inside him with the violence. He stood over Viggo, seeing him still for the first time. He wasn't dead, and he wasn't quite unconscious.

Jimmy steadied himself; every fiber was tingling with the power that had taken over. He was stuck, imprisoned in his own head, observing through two blue windows in a cell wall. He knelt down over Viggo. This was the moment to kill. And he was probably going to have to kill Yannick too.

Jimmy's right hand tensed up. His fingers squeezed together, ready to execute one fatal chop. The inner Jimmy wanted to scream. As of that moment he was filled with hatred for everything he was being made to do, and everyone who had put him there. His anger was stifled by his programming, but all the stronger because it couldn't get out. Into his mind flashed the faces of Dr. Higgins, Miss Bennett, and the monstrous sneer of Ares Hollingdale. Would it be easier to kill any of them? he wondered. His body was calm when it should have been panicking. His hand was steady when it should have been shaking.

This is wrong, he thought. I can't kill. But . . . I can't stop myself.

Jimmy raised his arm. His muscles gushed with the desire to end a life. "A single blow to the neck." The phrase haunted him now. Viggo's neck was stretched out, his head lying back on the floor. A soft groan slipped from his throat. His last one? Jimmy had to stop himself. Whatever the consequences, this was wrong.

The killer wasn't listening, though. Take control, Jimmy thought, over and over. He tried to say it, to shout it, but instead he felt his elbow straighten. His hand was coming down—the murderous weapon. *Take control*, he screamed inside his head.

The shadow of Jimmy's hand was across Viggo's face—then, his dazzling eyes sprang open. Jimmy's arm swung down with the force of an ax. Viggo saw it coming. With a final burst of strength he caught Jimmy's hand a centimeter from his throat. Jimmy, the assassin, wasn't giving up. He pulled his wrist out of Viggo's grip. Jimmy, the boy, still screamed silently to stop: *Take control*. Viggo knew what was going to happen, but he couldn't get away now.

Jimmy's hand was back at the top of its arc. This time he would crash through Viggo's defense. *Take control* ran through his head again. His tongue twitched, but his hand started to fall. It swept through the air with intent as Jimmy's mouth burst open.

Viggo couldn't move. He looked into his murderer's eyes and saw someone he had known long ago. There *was* humanity there. His final breath rushed out: "Helen . . ."

At the whisper of his mother's name, suddenly Jimmy sensed a bolt of color all over him.

"*Take control!*" he screamed. He felt alive again. His hand thudded hard into the floorboard, cracking the wood. The back of his fingers brushed Viggo's ear, and his hand slammed down, trapping Viggo's hair against the floor.

SAFFRON WALDEN

It took a long time for them both to recover. Jimmy was shaking. Images swirled around his head, and he held on to the floor of the restaurant as the world was spun out of control. It hardly registered when Christopher Viggo gathered himself and started tidying the furniture. Jimmy had only an impression of the man as he straightened the tables and neatly lined up every piece of cutlery. Then Jimmy sensed the man's shadow over him, still and cold. The silhouette stirred something deep inside Jimmy's memory. He felt a hand on his shoulder and remembered it was Viggo's, the man he was meant to kill—the man who might kill Jimmy now.

But he didn't. Instead he guided Jimmy to his feet and put an arm round his shoulders. They moved wordlessly through the kitchen, through another door, and up some dingy stairs into Viggo's apartment. It was dark outside, but a lamppost threw light in. There were no blinds, so it was only dimmed by the dirt on the windows. Jimmy looked out at the tops of the golden letters he had seen from the outside: IZGARU. He stared at them, still in a daze, while Viggo limped around the apartment—the fight had clearly done some damage. Eventually he sighed and rubbed the back of his neck as he eased himself into a tattered old armchair.

"You okay?" Viggo asked, his voice wavering a little for the first time. Then he grunted a tired laugh. "You're fine." He put his head back and balanced a bag of frozen peas on his forehead. "But look what you've done to me."

Jimmy found a seat to perch on. He studied the man as if it would unlock a mystery. He had never met anybody like this before. Viggo kept his eyes closed and rested his head under the frozen peas. Jimmy was glad not to feel the same aches and pains from the fight, but battles raged inside him. His stomach throbbed, and his thoughts were still cloudy. His programming wasn't giving up; it wanted to kill Viggo. It took all Jimmy's concentration to stay where he was.

"How do you know my mother?" he asked at last. He had been scared to speak until then. He was afraid that if he did, he would lose control and start trying to kill again.

"We were friends at MI6," said Viggo, "before you were born." Then he slowly lifted his head and took the peas away. "You have a sister, don't you?"

"Yeah. Georgie."

"Of course. I remember her as a baby. She must be, what, fourteen now?"

"She's thirteen."

"Thirteen, right. I left NJ7 just after she was born."

Jimmy scrutinized Viggo more closely. Much about him resembled Jimmy's father, but he was in better shape. He had more stubble too, and longer hair. Otherwise they were a similar size and build — it must be the look of all NJ7 agents.

"Why did you leave?" Jimmy was feeling bolder now as the troubles inside him softened.

"Ares Hollingdale is a maniac. He was a maniac even at NJ7, before he was prime minister. I saw it then, and he's become more powerful every day for fourteen years."

"Thirteen," Jimmy corrected him.

"Yes, thirteen." Viggo sighed heavily. His face looked suddenly tired. The lamplight drew weighty bags under his eyes. "Jimmy, do you know why you were sent to kill me?"

"For the good of the . . ." Jimmy trailed off. He didn't have the spirit to finish.

"Hollingdale came to power by eliminating all his opposition. He intimidated and exterminated anyone who stood in his way. Now, even if someone wants to dispute his absolute authority, there is no way of standing against him. He's taken control of the press, the TV, the radio; he controls when and where there is a vote, and he controls the outcome. Do you know how he does that, Jimmy?" Viggo was passionate now, his eyes searing into Jimmy's face. Jimmy was very much afraid that he knew the answer to Viggo's question.

"The Green Stripe," he said with a lump in his throat.

"That's right," said Viggo, rising and walking over to the window. "He uses the strength and technology of NJ7 to keep himself in power, while the country is starved of resources." He stared down onto the sidewalk. "Hollingdale must be stopped."

Jimmy could hear the restaurant below filling up with hungry customers.

"You're wrong," he urged. "People would never let him do it."

"Most people don't realize the extent of it," Viggo countered. "I told you—he controls what we hear. All the broadcasting and media companies have government agents high up in their organizations. Even people who can see what he's doing are too scared to put up a fight. He's a bully with a secret army, and his army will never disobey him. He made sure of that when he designed you."

"What? No, Dr. Higgins designed me."

"Dr. Higgins was on the team that designed you, Jimmy, and he's in charge of NJ7's technology now, but who do you think it was back then? Whose vision was brought into the world thirteen years ago? Ares Hollingdale's, of course."

"You mean eleven years ago—I'm eleven."

"Yes, silly of me. You're only eleven." He turned away and walked into the kitchen. But Viggo didn't sound like he had made another mistake. It was strange: Jimmy had reminded him a moment before exactly how much time had passed. And if Viggo left NJ7 thirteen years ago, thought Jimmy, how did he know about *him*, Jimmy Coates, who was only built eleven years ago? Something didn't add up.

Jimmy was about to question Viggo further, but there was a soft knock on the door. Then the most beautiful woman Jimmy had ever seen pushed it open and waited in the doorway. She could have been a Greek statue, except instead of being white marble, she was a deep and luxurious black. And if the goddesses that statues represented could walk, this was how they would enter a room. She moved as if her feet didn't need to touch the ground, gliding as smooth as honey. A ringlet of black hair played on her shoulder, and her eyes caught the orange light.

"Is this the boy Yannick told me to watch out for?" Her voice was exactly as it should have been—deep, mysterious, and musical. Christopher Viggo returned from the kitchen wiping his hands on a cloth. He smiled, and the two of them shared an awkward kiss. They weren't sure how to behave in front of Jimmy, the eleven-year-old assassin.

"Jimmy," said Viggo, sitting back in his armchair with a different packet of frozen vegetables, "this is Saffron." The stunning lady moved closer to Jimmy and held out her hand. Her fingers stretched out for miles.

"I'm Saffron Walden. Pleased to meet you."

"Hi; I'm Jimmy," he squeaked, taking her hand and shaking it roughly.

"Saffron runs the restaurant, Jimmy," Viggo explained from under his brussels sprouts, "and she's also helping with the cause."

Saffron moved over to Viggo, her midnight-blue cocktail dress swishing as she went.

"Yannick's taken quite a beating," she said, "but he'll fix you something when he gets a chance. It's not too busy tonight."

Jimmy hoped the restaurant's kitchen was cleaner than the rest of the place. The apartment certainly hadn't been tidied up for a long time. There were papers and books lying in haphazard piles all over the floor, the bed in the corner was unmade, and covering everything was a layer of dust to match the stains on the windows.

"What are we going to do with him?" Saffron asked, looking straight at Jimmy. Her head was tilted slightly to one side, which emphasized the elegant curve of her neck.

"I think the question is: What does he want to do with us?"

Viggo replied. "He could kill us both right now if he wanted to." That comment hurt Jimmy. It may have been true, but Viggo didn't realize how much Jimmy was straining to hold himself back. His muscles were seething, his teeth clenched. His programming was still urging him to kill. When Jimmy didn't reply, Viggo softened his tone. "How much control do you have over your skills?"

"I don't know. More than I did at first, I guess. I'm getting more in control all the time. But the powers are getting stronger too."

"I think that's the way it works. By the time you're eighteen, the assassin is meant to have completely replaced the person. Until then, you're in danger."

"Danger?" Jimmy echoed.

"When Hollingdale finds out you didn't kill me," said Viggo, avoiding eye contact, "he'll need to kill you. NJ7 will track you down, and your family, and your friends."

"But—he already has my parents." Jimmy felt as if an ice bullet had pierced his lungs.

"I see." Viggo glanced at Saffron. "Don't worry; we can help you. And having you on our side will help us, of course." Jimmy looked at him anxiously. "But first we'll have to rescue your parents."

A smile crept onto Jimmy's face, but before Viggo could say anything more, there was a loud bang and Yannick entered, filling the door frame with his bulk. He had kicked open the door, a full plate in each hand. In he lumbered and unceremoniously plonked one of the plates on the table in front of Jimmy, the other in Viggo's hands. Both were covered in a mountain of green slop. Then Yannick trudged into the flat's tiny kitchen and emerged with two forks. Still without a word, he tossed one over to Jimmy, and it landed next to the plate. With the other he stole a mouthful from Viggo's plate and guzzled it down.

"Cabbage." He grunted, chewing a second mouthful. Jimmy picked at the gunk on his plate.

"You used to do better than cabbage, Yannick," Viggo said with a chuckle. "One of my little indulgences when I was still at MI6, Jimmy, was lunch at the Savoy Hotel."

"You were the scruffiest customer I ever cooked for," Yannick declared, as if it were the result of a competition. There was a strange lilt to his accent. French? thought Jimmy. Or maybe it was Turkish. But without saying anything else, Yannick was out the door and heading back to work.

A moment later Viggo's expression had turned solemn again. "Can they trace you?" he asked, deadly serious.

"I don't think so," Jimmy replied, eventually. "They had enough trouble finding me when I was running away from them."

"That makes sense. After all, what's the point of top secret, state-of-the-art military technology that's easy to find? And you weren't followed?" Viggo pressed.

"No. Well, I don't think so. They said I was designed to work alone."

"Good. Then we have a little time. Sleep here tonight. We have at least until morning before NJ7 realizes what's happened."

When the sun made it impossible to sleep any more, Jimmy picked himself out of bed and shook off the latest elusive nightmares. Viggo had slept on the floor, but he was already up, half dressed in an old T-shirt and a pair of boxer shorts. His hair was as crumpled as his shirt, and his face had sprouted another layer of stubble.

"The bathroom is downstairs. Sorry it's a bit grubby."

Jimmy had expected nothing less.

In the next half hour, both Saffron and Yannick let themselves in. Yannick brought a bag of fresh pastries, and Saffron moved some of the mess so that there was room for all of them to sit down.

The rest of the day was spent planning. They sat round the rickety old table, while Yannick kept them well supplied with refreshments. Jimmy found that he loved watching Christopher Viggo think. The man rarely stayed in his seat for long. He would run both his hands through his hair and stand up, then pace the room, growling out ideas, facts, instructions. He concocted wild plans that grew and grew, then threw each of them out, furious at himself, before he struck on the seed of the next scheme. He wanted to know every single detail about Jimmy's stay underground at NJ7.

"Yes, they've expanded it since I was there," he said, his voice calm, but his eyes wild with concentration. "And they changed all the ways in and out as soon as I left. Jimmy, the only three entrances you saw were the one in the river, the one in the back of the tailor's, and the one inside Number Ten, Downing Street, right?"

"That's right."

"So that's what we have to go on." Viggo stopped at the window and stared out.

Saffron was scribbling down notes on thick pads of paper.

She paused for a second and put the pencil to her lips.

"The tailor's could be any one of hundreds. If the underground complex is really that big, we might never find that particular shop." She stared at Viggo's back.

"You're right. But it's worth looking. Tell Yannick what he's looking for and to get on it." Saffron scrawled a note with Viggo's instruction. Then he was off again: "Jimmy, who, apart from your parents, knows what's happened to you?"

Jimmy thought about Felix. An image of him being shot with a dart nagged at his mind. He didn't know what had happened to his friend after that. Equally, he had no idea whether his sister was okay. Had she been handed over to NJ7 too? Or was NJ7 happy to leave her with that horrible Doren family?

"Georgie and Felix," Jimmy announced. His insides quivered, but this time it wasn't his programming. This time it was an instinct he knew he wanted more than anything to act on. "We have to find them before NJ7 knows what I've done."

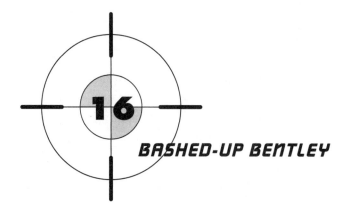

16

BASHED-UP BENTLEY

Viggo drove as if he was being chased. He flicked through the gears like he was conducting an orchestra, whisking them through the night toward the Dorens' house. Jimmy sat in the back and checked his seat belt after every swerve.

"What do you think of the car, Jimmy?" Viggo shouted from the front seat, sounding unusually excited. It was a beautiful car, but in terrible condition; it was an old indigo Bentley—far too posh to be in keeping with everything else about Christopher Viggo.

"It's nice. I've never been in a Bentley before," Jimmy yelled back.

The dark leather seats were impressive, but Jimmy was more concerned with the way Viggo was driving. In the front passenger seat, Saffron appeared quite used to the ordeal. She didn't flinch when Viggo steamed through a red light at double the speed limit; she barely winced as the rear of the car knocked over a row of garbage cans when Viggo skidded round a tight corner.

"It used to belong to the French ambassador." Viggo grinned at Jimmy, taking his eye off the road a fraction too long for comfort. "But it was confiscated by MI6." Saffron reached across and corrected the steering wheel, as London's nighttime streets flashed by. "They found secret compartments in it that were used to smuggle documents in and out of the country."

"I thought the French were our allies," Jimmy said.

Viggo grunted a quick laugh. "They are." He snorted. "But Ares Hollingdale has something against them. The documents were planted."

"So what did the French government do?"

"What could they do?" said Viggo with a shrug. "The old ambassador was sent back to Paris, and Hollingdale's just waiting for an excuse to get rid of the new one too. He hates all foreigners, but he hates the French most of all."

One question struck Jimmy. "So, if MI6 confiscated the car, how come you have it?"

Viggo hesitated just long enough for Saffron to snort. "He stole it."

"I did not steal it!" Viggo was indignant, and put his foot down to take the next corner even faster than the others. Saffron just raised an eyebrow.

"Okay," he admitted, crunching the car up another gear, "when I left NJ7, I needed something to drive, plus I thought there might be some documents left in it."

"I thought you said the documents were planted?"

"They were, but after the car was confiscated, Hollingdale had agents searching it for months. They never found anything, but it was obvious he genuinely thought there was something else hidden in it."

The car screeched into an alley barely wide enough for it.

"But don't worry," Viggo added. "I know how to disguise a vehicle."

Then Saffron cut in, "Do you know where you're going?" Her voice juddered with the car.

"I'm going straight to the address Jimmy gave me."

Viggo did seem confident about where he was going. It was as if he had all the streets of London imprinted on his memory. His route took in side streets, back alleys, stretches of road that weren't really even road. He took shortcuts through parking lots, shopping centers, and pedestrian precincts. Hardly a second was spent on any main road. Which was just as well, because at that speed, the police would definitely have pulled him over.

They arrived at the Dorens' street sooner than Jimmy expected. Now Viggo slowed the car to a crawl, the engine purring with stately dignity. He killed the headlights.

"These guys must be doing all right; look at the size of these houses!" said Saffron, turning her neck as they drifted past each.

Viggo's response was immediate. "Hollingdale's supporters tend to do all right these days."

The car pulled up outside the Dorens' gate. The gravel driveway beyond was floodlit; the ground floor was probably alarmed at night. The house was a domestic fortress.

"Time to abduct your sister, Jimmy," said Viggo in a hush.

The eerie atmosphere of suburbia in the small hours seeped into the car. Viggo shut off the engine.

"Wait here," he whispered. He pulled a scarf out of his pocket and wrapped it round his hand. From under the seat he picked up a thick black blanket, but he caught Jimmy's worried expression. "I'm not going to hurt her, but I don't want her to scream. Okay?"

Jimmy nodded. Viggo reached over to Saffron and patted her warmly on the arm. "If I'm not back in two minutes, drive away. If you hear an alarm, drive away. If anybody comes out of the house except me and Georgie, drive away. Got it? Just go. I'll find my way back to you."

"Let me come too," Jimmy said with a gasp, but Viggo was already gone, a shadow fading into shadows.

"Don't worry," Saffron said. "He knows what he's doing."

The time passed achingly slowly. The car's old-fashioned clock ticked off the seconds, each one a twist in Jimmy's guts, each one another drop of sweat teasing down his cheek. Saffron was just as nervous as he was. They watched the clock. Jimmy's head was racing with uncertainty. He'd warned Viggo about all the rooms, but what if he stumbled on Eva's parents by mistake? What if one of Eva's brothers had come home for the night?

Each tick boomed another second. One minute left. Jimmy couldn't stand it.

"He'll never do it." He gasped. "He needs more time!" Fifty seconds left. Saffron turned in her seat. Her beautiful brown face looked pale in the darkness.

"Two minutes, Jimmy. One hundred twenty seconds. He means it. If we sit here any longer, there's a risk we'll be spotted. NJ7 knows me; they know this house. If they see us parked here and make the connection, we're all dead." Thirty seconds to go. Jimmy's eyes never left the clock. "If Chris can't find her in two minutes, he'll come out. If he isn't out in two minutes, he's dead."

Twenty seconds of agony left. Nothing in the night stirred. Ten seconds. Something hit the corner of Jimmy's eye. He whipped his head round. A bush rustled. Was Viggo coming back? Had he done it? A fox trotted exquisitely across the road.

Saffron edged her door open and strode round the front of the car to slip into the driver's seat. The keys were in the ignition. Jimmy wanted to stop her. Her fingers quivered on the key. Jimmy's eyes darted from the house to Saffron to the clock.

"It's time," she announced, and started the engine.

"Wait!" Silhouetted against the security light, a strong figure strode forward. The Bentley snarled its readiness. Viggo broke into a run. He was carrying a person in his arms, like the knight carries the princess away from the dragon, except this princess was wrapped in a blanket with a scarf tightly wound around her mouth.

Saffron reached across and pushed open the passenger door. Viggo burst in, the bundle on his lap.

"Go!" He panted. Saffron calmly slipped the car away from the house. "Sorry I was late," Viggo continued. "So many damn rooms in that house."

The bundle in Viggo's arms was struggling. Now that they were safely away, he loosened his grip and untied the scarf.

"Hey! Let me go!" she screamed, piercing the tranquility of the motor's hum.

Jimmy recognized the voice and pulled himself out of his seat to stare—at Eva Doren.

"Where's my sister?" he exclaimed.

Viggo looked at him sharply. "What do you mean?"

"Jimmy!" Eva had seen him at last. "What's going on?" She kicked out, causing Saffron to swerve slightly. Jimmy didn't answer her. Instead he shouted at Viggo.

"This is the wrong girl!"

"What? This is the only girl there was."

"This isn't my sister. This is Eva Doren."

"Oh, you're kidding, right?"

"No, he is not kidding," Eva shouted. She looked up at Viggo from his lap. "Hey, I know you. You're—" Her mood suddenly shifted. The muscles in her face relaxed, and something tender slipped into her expression. She looked a little dopey. "You're Christopher Viggo," she mewed softly. Viggo pushed her over into the backseat.

Jimmy was distraught. He didn't like Eva at the best of times. Now she'd probably try to call the police, her parents, or even NJ7. "Turn round; we have to put Eva back and get Georgie."

Saffron kept going, though, speeding up until she was driving almost as fast as Viggo.

"Georgie's not at my house," snapped Eva.

"Shut up, will you?" Jimmy was furious. "You've already ruined everything once. It's your fault I got caught."

"That's rubbish. I had nothing to do with that."

"You lured me to your house, then drugged me and called the police."

"That wasn't me, I swear." Eva glanced between Viggo and Jimmy. "Do you think my parents told me what they were doing? I would have told Georgie, wouldn't I? She would never have brought you back to my house if she knew."

Jimmy was silenced, but he still felt uneasy about trusting her. She reminded him too much of her mother.

Saffron provided the voice of reason. "Eva, tell us where

Georgie is, then we'll take you back to bed."

"Don't!" Jimmy shouted. "She'll tell her parents everything, and that will be it."

"I would never do that."

Viggo couldn't stand the bickering anymore.

"Shut up, would you! Both of you! Now listen to me, Eva, did they take Georgie when they took Jimmy?" Jimmy's throat tightened. "Where is Georgie?"

Eva was shaking her head in anger. "They only just managed to take Jimmy, what with all the fuss she made." Jimmy and Viggo looked at her inquisitively. "She has a violent streak," Eva explained. "It took three other men to drag her away. But they took her somewhere else, I think."

The Bentley rumbled on at fierce speed, and Eva revealed her terms. "If you let me come with you, Mr. Viggo, I'll tell you what I know about where Georgie is."

"Come with us to get Georgie, you mean?" Viggo said. His voice was settling back to its natural coolness.

"Obviously that. But we thought Jimmy was locked up somewhere, and instead he's here, which means you're helping him. And I've seen you on the news. You're like an outlaw or something." She made her eyes as big as they would go. "So listen, I want to find Georgie with you, but then I want to go with you and help with whatever you're planning." Her request was met with confusion. "So is it a deal?"

Eva grinned, far too chirpy for a girl who had just been kidnapped by accident.

"Look, we're not planning anything, okay?" Viggo said, avoiding Eva's adoring gaze. "We're just looking after Jimmy."

"Fine. So I'll look after Jimmy with you. And Georgie of

course." There was a long pause. "But don't make me go home. My parents have been going on and on—the *wonderful* government, the *marvelous* prime minister, the *simply super* police force. I can't stand it!"

Jimmy was amazed at Eva's perfect impression of her mother.

"Just tell us what you know." Viggo sighed.

"But it's a deal, right?" she insisted.

Jimmy couldn't stand any more. "Fine!" he blasted. "You can come with us as long as you stop whining."

"Brilliant! Okay, when they took Georgie, they said something about the 'Ms. Becky' house. I think it's, like, code for something."

If he hadn't been so worried, Jimmy would have laughed—NJ7 had obviously taken her to the Muzbekes' house. He was so relieved he almost hugged Eva.

"But she's not answering her phone or replying to my text messages," she continued. "Anyway, that's all I know." She crossed her arms, burying herself in the blanket, and turned her head haughtily to look out the window.

"That's where we were going next anyway!" said Jimmy. "It's the Muzbekes' house." Saffron and Viggo had obviously worked it out too, as Saffron hadn't let the car's speed drop for a moment. "All that stupid arguing," Jimmy cried, "and we're on our way to get Felix anyway!"

"Well, I didn't know that, did I?"

"You're so annoying."

Saffron let out a deep breath. "Would you two shut up? I'm trying to drive here. Now listen, Eva, is Felix okay? Jimmy says he was shot by a tranquilizer dart."

Eva screwed up her face in response. "What? How would I know? I've never met Felix."

At the speed they were going, they soon reached the Muzbekes' house.

Saffron cut the lights and slowed to a crawl. But Viggo was uneasy.

"It's too risky," he whispered. "If they're with Felix's family, then they're safe, and we don't want to take them away with us, do we?"

"Sure we do," said Jimmy. "They'll help us."

Viggo rolled his eyes. "I'm not running a youth training scheme, you know. What am I going to do with a bunch of kids 'helping'? No. We shouldn't be here. Turn the car round."

"What?" Jimmy was shocked, but Saffron was already shifting into reverse.

"I'm not doing anything stupid." The conversation was over for Viggo.

Then Eva piped up. "I'll go."

Saffron stopped the car. Viggo turned round.

"I'll ring the bell. It won't be suspicious. I know it's the middle of the night, but I can make something up—my house is on fire, or I'm sleepwalking, or I ran away. That last one's almost true, isn't it?"

The only response was stunned silence. Before anyone could react, Eva had jumped out. "If everything's okay, I'll signal to you, like this." She stuck two fingers in her mouth and blew out a faint squeal. "No wait." She stopped herself. "If everything's okay, I'll just shout, 'Okay.' But if it isn't, *then* I'll whistle."

She'd rattled off her instructions before Viggo could tell her what a bad idea it was. The car door slammed shut, and Eva pulled her blanket around her as she padded, barefoot, over the road.

"She's still in her pajamas, for God's sake!" Viggo huffed.

Saffron was less put out. "Well none of *us* can go, can we? Not with NJ7 after us."

The three of them sat in the car, peering into the darkness. Viggo didn't stop complaining. "This is no way to run an operation. She hasn't even given a two-minute cutoff."

Eva stopped outside the front gate and stared up the driveway. Everything was still. Surely nobody was watching the house. If they were, they were well hidden. She walked up to the front door and pushed the bell firmly. The hall light came on. The front door swung open.

From inside the car Jimmy could only just make out what was happening. He saw the door open and watched Eva raise her head to talk.

But something was wrong. Jimmy could see a suit and tie through the leaves. The porch light picked out the shape of a white shirt under a dark jacket. Why was Neil Muzbeke wearing a suit at this time of night? Jimmy would always remember him in a woman's bathrobe.

"That's not Felix's dad," Jimmy whispered.

Saffron and Viggo snapped their heads round to look at him.

"That's NJ7."

BAD CITIZENS

Saffron hurled the car forward.

"We can't just leave her!" Jimmy cried.

"We should never have come," snarled Viggo.

Jimmy knew what he had to do. He thrust open the car door. With the road screaming along beneath him, Jimmy unclipped his seat belt and dove out. He hit the asphalt and rolled away from the vehicle. As the brakes screeched, he smacked his palms onto the road to stop himself, then pushed himself onto his feet. He was buzzing now. His programming had kicked in. Had he called it? Or had it responded to his jumping out of the car? Jimmy wasn't sure.

Now he was running. Dead fast. He cut through the wind, heading straight for the Muzbekes' front door. Eva was still standing there, chatting happily away to a tall, broad man in a black suit. His deep-set eyes flicked up, and Jimmy knew he had been spotted. He could almost make out the muscles twitch beneath the man's shirt.

Saffron spun the car around. Not caring now how much noise they made, or how conspicuous they were, she flashed on the lights and drove straight at the house, mounting the sidewalk. The headlights dazzled the man in the doorway, who shielded his eyes. Eva screamed. It definitely wasn't the "Okay" signal.

The man reached for his gun, but Jimmy saw his fingers move. He hurled himself forward. Eva screamed again as Jimmy jumped right over her. His shoulder struck the man's face just as the gun came free from its holster. They tumbled to the ground. One shot shrieked out.

Viggo ran from the car and plucked Eva off the ground under his arm. Jimmy was up and facing another man in the hall. Jimmy's arms swung like deadly pendulums, blocking the man's punches. Then he lashed out with his heel and knocked the gun out of the man's holster. Jimmy heaved him over his head and clubbed him down on top of the first man, who was too slow to get out of the way. Both were knocked unconscious.

Felix and Georgie were standing halfway up the stairs, openmouthed.

"Jimmy!" they shouted together, and ran to embrace him.

"What on earth are you wearing?" said Felix, laughing at Jimmy's silky shirt. Viggo was still carrying Eva, but ready to pounce.

"Who else is here?" he shouted. "Are there more of them?"

"That's it," Georgie answered. "There were only two of them."

"Then let's get out of here. Felix, are your parents here?"

"No," said Felix, his laugh suddenly withering, leaving his face uncharacteristically serious. Viggo stepped over the two

NJ7 agents and marched out the door.

"Put me down!" shouted Eva from under Viggo's arm.

"Not until we're back in the car."

Viggo threw her roughly into the backseat, and she let out a little yelp. The others piled in after her, squashing up to fit all four of them in. Viggo slammed his door closed.

"Four kids in their pajamas. Honestly."

"I'm in uniform," Jimmy angrily pointed out.

"You should never have gone in to get them!" Viggo was enraged, but Jimmy was flaming too.

"You were just going to drive away!"

"We should have done."

"Well, why didn't you? They're my friends, and you don't have to look after me."

"I wasn't going to let you get yourself killed, was I?"

"But it's okay to leave these three in the hands of NJ7, is it?" Jimmy felt violence still running through his veins. "For all we knew, they were dead."

"So we could have been risking our lives for nothing, couldn't we?" Viggo didn't turn to look at Jimmy, but he knew that was the last word.

Jimmy's programming hummed inside him. Now that it had been woken up, he felt the evil, organic machine part of him creeping through his brain. He had hazy visions of throwing his arm round Viggo's neck and strangling him there and then.

He gritted his teeth and shook his head, then turned to his friends. The tension was still in his voice when he spoke.

"It's great to see you," he said.

"Thanks for coming for us." Georgie beamed, affectionately squeezing Jimmy's shoulder. Eva squirmed round in her seat and wrapped her arms around Georgie.

"I'm so pleased to see you!" she trilled.

Viggo wasn't so relaxed. "Saffron, you better step on it," he said.

"I am stepping on it."

"Well, step on it harder."

There were two cars chasing them. Saffron powered the Bentley through the same confusion of side streets. Like Viggo, she seemed to know exactly where to turn. The four passengers in the back were squashed together every time the car swung to either side. The speed was building, but the two black cars were close behind.

"They're catching up," Viggo cried, opening his window and adjusting the side mirror so that he could see behind. "Two cars. Definitely NJ7."

"Who else would be following us?" Saffron shouted over the roar of the wind.

Viggo's face fell. "It's no good," he bellowed. "They'll have air support any second now. We can't get away from helicopters."

Saffron glanced across at him and smiled. "Of course we can." She lurched the steering wheel round the next corner, and Felix was first to realize where she was heading.

"No way, you can't drive onto the—" But they were already at the subway station. The car crashed through the flimsy metal fence onto the platform. It was a suburban station, so they weren't underground, and underground was where they needed to be. Saffron accelerated to the end of the raised platform, then wrenched the steering wheel across. They soared onto the tracks, landing with a bump.

Now the journey was as rough as it could be. Two wheels were up on a smooth metal track, but the other two were staggering over the wooden sleepers.

"What if there's a train?" shouted Georgie, her voice vibrating with the car.

"There won't be any trains at this time of night," Saffron called back.

Viggo checked the mirror. Both the NJ7 cars had followed them through the station and onto the track.

"Can't we go any faster?" he shouted.

"We've never had so many people in this car before, Chris," said Saffron. Then the rattling of the wooden slats beneath them blended with a swift but steady *chop-chop-chop*. Viggo didn't need to look up. The sound alone told him a swarm of helicopters was preparing to fire.

"They're charging their rockets," he bellowed. "If they hit, we've had it."

"What do you want me to do about that, genius?" Saffron replied. The needle on the speedometer was straining at the top of the dial. They plunged toward the tunnel.

Suddenly, the sky lit up with a faint orange. Jimmy knew what that was. He had flown one of those helicopters and he had fired the rockets. Then he heard a piercing whistle, like a child's scream.

The tunnel swallowed them just in time, but the chasing cars were still following. The rocket blasted into the stonework above them, and a fountain of golden flames erupted all over the track. The force of the explosion threw one of the black cars behind them high into the air. It flipped over and landed with a sad crumple.

The Bentley was immersed in darkness now, until the only black car to make it through the explosion burst its lights on. The cavernous channel amplified the roar of the two engines.

Suddenly, flashing by so fast they nearly missed it, was the platform of the next station. The remaining NJ7 car was centimeters away now, edging closer as they hurtled through the underground at breakneck speed.

"Hold on, everyone," said Saffron. Her fingers hung loosely off the steering wheel, cool as could be. Jimmy could just make out the light of the next station filtering down the tunnel toward them. Saffron rammed her foot down on the brake. The Bentley skidded all the way along the track into the station. The car behind hadn't had enough time to brake, and they were clashing bumpers now. Then Saffron jerked the wheel to one side. The front of the car caught under the stone edging of the platform.

The car behind was still surging forward. It shunted the back of the Bentley into the air, sending it tumbling over itself, until they were completely upside down. Someone screamed; Jimmy thought it must have been Eva. They were thrown up from their seats as the car kept twisting, and flipped over completely. It came down with a thud the right way up, sitting on the platform.

"That was so cool," announced Felix, pushing his hair out of his face.

The driver of the NJ7 car had no idea what had happened. By the time he had reversed back to the station, Saffron had driven with precision through a pedestrian walkway and across to the other platform. There, the Bentley gathered speed and dove onto the other track with a bounce; they started back in the opposite direction—toward the open air.

"Wait a minute," said Felix quickly. "We've crossed over to the Northern Line."

"Exactly." Saffron smirked. "The helicopters might wait forever for us to come out, but they'll be at the wrong exit. Meanwhile, we'll reach Finchley mostly underground."

Viggo reached across the car and squeezed Saffron's knee. "Good driving," he said with a quiet smile.

Felix was bouncing up and down in his seat. "Jimmy, you rescued us," he said. "Those men were from some kind of secret police and they—"

"Yeah, I know," Jimmy interrupted him.

"But they came last night and took away my parents." Felix suddenly stopped bouncing and slowed down when he saw that everyone was listening to him. "They came to the house, and put Mum and Dad in the back of a van." Jimmy hadn't been expecting this. "The men said they should have been loyal to the government, and that they should have turned you in, Jimmy." There was a volatile hush in the car between each of Felix's words. "They called them 'bad citizens.'"

After a long pause Viggo turned round and looked into Felix's face. "Do you know where they took them?" he asked in his deep monotone.

"No. But then these two other men came in—the ones that you beat up, Jimmy." A hint of a smile slithered along Felix's lips, but then vanished. "They said they were going to look after me and Georgie until they could find us some decent parents." He dropped his gaze to his lap and held it there.

"They didn't even realize that I'm not his sister," Georgie added, almost indignant, "and they wouldn't let us out of the house, and they wouldn't let us use the phone."

Viggo looked across at Saffron, the lines on his forehead as deep as the underground line they were driving along. She didn't look back at him, though; she was concentrating on the track. Jimmy saw a sadness in the corner of her eye that hadn't been there before.

Jimmy stared out the window. He wondered what would happen to Neil and Olivia Muzbeke. He had never thanked them for looking after him. The last time he saw them, they had been facedown on the carpet in their front hall and he had taken them for traitors. He remembered how angry he had been when he thought Felix's mum had called the police. Now he knew that not only had they helped him, but that they were paying a price for it. The misfortune was spreading, and he felt like it was all flowing out from him.

"I hope Yannick has cooked us up some grub. I'm starving." Viggo stretched his arms out in front of him and rolled his head from side to side. Saffron was gently easing the car into a discreet garage next door to Izgaru. The automatic doors devoured them.

Sure enough, Yannick was in the restaurant kitchen. He was the same as ever. His apron looked like it was made entirely of grease; his bulging belly was testimony to his love of his job.

Jimmy's eyes, along with those of Felix, Eva, and Georgie, had jumped to the work surfaces of the kitchen. Yannick had laid out a glorious feast. Even Viggo and Saffron were stunned by what they saw.

There were piles of kebabs, huge platters full of schwarmas, dolmas, buckets of couscous, ezme, olives, and several bowls full of kisir.

"You've been busy," quipped Viggo, heading straight for a lamb kebab.

"I get nervous when you guys go out to cause trouble," said Yannick, "so I cook."

"There was no need to be *this* nervous, Yannick."

It was a midnight feast long after midnight. They all stuffed their faces as if they were never going to eat again. They drank real Coke. It could only have come from the black market.

Jimmy was elated that Georgie and Felix were okay. And it was probably best that Eva wasn't dead either. It was brilliant to be messing around with Felix again. He and Jimmy ate more than the others, and Felix still managed to crack stupid jokes between mouthfuls. He had even memorized a song he'd found on the Internet, about Hollingdale wishing everything in the world could be British, and Eva joined in on the less rude bits.

Georgie kept trying to knock food out of Jimmy's hands. She hadn't done that since they were little. Jimmy laughed and tried it on her. Then Felix started juggling falafel, and Yannick decided to throw the stuffed peppers at him.

It was only later, as dawn licked the remains of the food, when they were all dropping off to sleep on the floor of the kitchen, holding their bursting bellies, that Jimmy realized something was different about his friend. Even for Felix, the jokes and tricks were over the top, when really he was hiding a deep sadness.

Jimmy looked across at him. Felix was asleep, and the smile that usually defined his face was gone. Was he dreaming of his parents? Jimmy knew very well what it was like to worry about parents. He reached for a dry tea towel, rolled it up, and propped it behind his friend's head.

Jimmy woke up with Viggo whispering in his ear, "You have to come with us now."

"What time is it?" He groaned.

"Afternoon. Let's get going."

"Where?" Jimmy stretched out. His neck was stiff from sleeping propped up against the kitchen wall. Felix was still asleep next to him. On the other side of the counter, Eva and Georgie had fallen asleep leaning on each other. The food mess had all been cleared. The kitchen was sparkling.

"NJ7 headquarters, of course."

Suddenly Jimmy was fully awake. His nightmare slipped away, like they always did. More training, he wondered, or just last night's spicy food?

"Come on, Jimmy," said Viggo. "We can leave your friends with Yannick. Maybe they can learn to wait tables."

Viggo looked refreshed and surprisingly tidy—as if the night before hadn't affected him at all. He had greased his hair back and sheared a fraction of a millimeter off his stubble. A crisp white shirt emphasized his robust physique, and his black trousers had two vertical creases that looked like they were keeping his legs straight.

Something sharpened Jimmy's nerves. Viggo moved to the other side of the kitchen. He turned his back to Jimmy and stared into the reflective surface of the ventilation fan above one of the ovens. He meticulously placed a tie round his collar. It was a long, thin, black tie. Jimmy knew where he had seen those before. When it was neatly tied and tight up to the nape of his neck, Viggo turned round. He silently picked up a suit jacket from the kitchen counter. A black jacket with a green stripe.

INTO THE DARK

Jimmy's mouth dropped open. Viggo looked like all the other NJ7 agents. The ones Jimmy had run away from.

"What's the matter?" Viggo had seen the look of horror on his face. Jimmy's words wouldn't come out properly. His throat had seized up, and inside him the killing instinct was stirring. "Jimmy, what's up? It's okay, this is my old NJ7 suit."

Jimmy tried to calm himself. Viggo had told him that he used to work for NJ7, but he still hadn't expected to see the uniform. "Why are you wearing it?" Jimmy gasped.

"I'll explain on the way. Come on," Viggo implored, but Jimmy wasn't moving. "Trust me, this is the best way for us to get close to NJ7."

Viggo was still whispering, anxious not to wake up the others. Jimmy breathed deeply, struggling to dissolve the hateful feeling inside him. Should he go with Viggo, or run?

The man was a mystery to him. None of Miss Bennett's data had prepared Jimmy for the quiet magnetism of Viggo's manner. Jimmy's head cleared for a second when his gut told him to ask for advice, but the one person who would have been able to help was the very man standing in front of him. Viggo himself had so quickly become Jimmy's only guide to this new and dangerous world. Where did that leave him now?

"I'll only come if the others come too," Jimmy declared, thinking on his feet.

"This lot?" Viggo balked. "They're not fighters. They're not trained like you and me." Viggo ran his hand over his hair. "Look, even Yannick isn't coming with us. He would be a liability. This lot would be . . . suicide."

"If you don't want them with us, then you don't have to come. But *I'm* going, and I'm taking them with me." Jimmy was stern, looking Viggo straight in the eye.

"Jimmy," pleaded Viggo, "don't you trust me?"

Jimmy scrutinized Viggo. The tie was hanging down from his neck a little crookedly—like a question mark.

"Felix," Jimmy shouted, "we're going on a mission."

"Now that you're here, just obey one simple instruction," Viggo announced as they sat down on the train. He leaned forward to conspire with them. "Do everything I say, and don't lose sight of me."

"That's two instructions," Eva pointed out.

Viggo turned on her. "I'm not responsible for you, okay? You shouldn't be here." He glanced at Jimmy, then back at the others. "So if you get killed, it's your own fault." He sat back in his seat, and Saffron gave him a disapproving look. He shrugged and tried to look innocent.

Georgie, Eva, and Felix were now dressed in old T-shirts

and trousers that Viggo had hacked off at the knee. They fit right in on the subway. Jimmy felt so conspicuous—still in his shiny black shirt. He wished that the green stripe was the logo of some big company, or at least a soccer team.

Felix was quiet. He leaned over to Jimmy and spoke right into his ear, to be above the volume of the train, but so that the others couldn't hear him. "Do you think my parents will be there?"

Jimmy looked straight ahead at his strange double reflection in the train window. "I'm not sure. It might be harder to find them. We know my mum and dad are there because they used to . . . they work there."

"They work for them?" Felix didn't sound all that surprised. Jimmy just nodded solemnly. He hadn't come to terms with it himself. It didn't help that Felix accepted it so calmly. "Does Georgie know?"

Jimmy didn't really hear what Felix had said, but he knew anyway.

"I haven't told her yet."

"Hadn't you better tell her before we get there? It's one thing freeing prisoners, but it's another thing trying to free the prison guards." Felix was quite pleased with his words of wisdom. He repeated them to himself, but then a thought struck him. "Hey, maybe your parents are guarding my parents. Then everything will be okay."

Jimmy let himself laugh a little.

"Thanks for coming with me, Felix."

They got off the train at Tottenham Court Road. Viggo and Saffron had been whispering to each other all the way. Were they still working out details of the plan? Jimmy thought they were probably just deciding what to do with the extra kids they had acquired. He was starting to feel foolish for insisting the others come along. Georgie would probably be okay. After all, she had already escaped Paduk once—and Felix was up for anything. But Eva? She wasn't suited to this sort of thing at all.

She kept complaining as they walked up New Oxford Street: about the clothes she was being made to wear, and about how far they were walking. Jimmy tried to blank out her voice, but it was hard because she talked louder than anybody else.

"She's so annoying," Jimmy whispered to Felix.

"She's *your* sister."

"Not her—Eva. She's only here because she doesn't want to go home and have to put up with her parents. They're even more annoying than she is."

"I don't mind her, but she does have a funny walk." Eva, Georgie, and Felix were all in borrowed shoes. Felix had managed to dig out a pair of Viggo's sneakers that weren't too bad once he had stuffed couscous into the toes, and Georgie had quite big feet anyway, so she was reasonably comfortable in a pair of Saffron's shoes. Eva, however, was struggling to put one foot in front of the other. She had refused to stuff her shoes with couscous, despite Felix's helpful suggestions. She had used tissue paper instead, which didn't mold to the shape of her foot like couscous would have.

Soon they were at Holborn station. Viggo stopped at the entrance to the station and brushed the side of his foot against a drain cover. Saffron saw Jimmy studying Viggo's movements and moved over to him.

"Can you see the letters on the manhole cover?"

Jimmy looked closer. He had seen covers like this everywhere. They all had letters on them, but Jimmy had never really looked at them before.

"It's code," Saffron continued. "The letters tell you which secret service operations and units should be operating in this street. And below it."

"So it doesn't just lead to the drains?"

"Some of them do, but this one definitely doesn't. This is Kingsway." She pointed up to the street sign as if it should mean something to Jimmy. It just looked like another street sign partly obscured by decades of grime from car exhausts. "It looks like this one has been sealed off. We'll have to go back underground."

Viggo made a quick gesture to the subway station entrance. They all followed him down.

"Back onto the tube? Are you sure this is right, Chris?" Eva was really starting to drive Jimmy mad. Why didn't Viggo tell her to shut up?

As they all jogged down the stairs, Viggo sidled up to Jimmy. He continually scanned their surroundings while he spoke.

"There's a disused tram tunnel underneath us. It runs all the way from Kingsway to Embankment, parallel to the tube line. And if what you say about the expansion of NJ7 HQ is right, it must run somewhere close to it."

"How do you know about it?" Jimmy thought he saw a strange smile creep into Viggo's eyes.

"Before they sealed up the manhole —," he started, but then interrupted himself. "No, it's nothing."

Jimmy stopped walking down the stairs. "What is it? Just tell me how you know."

Viggo definitely smiled now. "Jimmy, I used to bring dates here."

Jimmy's impatience was diffused into embarrassment. He tried not to show it by dropping his head and walking on.

The subway was overrun, as always. It may not have been rush hour, but still the people swarmed around the ticket machines and buzzed through the stiles. The clack of the machinery and all the hubbub made discreet instructions inaudible, so Viggo was using only the sparsest of sign language. They followed him in single file through the ticket gate and down the escalator. Everywhere Jimmy looked, there were faces that he thought were watching him. Eyes that he thought studied his face were actually just reading the ads behind his head. The leering wrinkles of Ares Hollingdale peered out at him, and only him, from the front of someone's evening paper. Another headline about how wonderful he was.

When they reached the platform, Viggo looked confused.

"I've never had to come in this way before," he explained to Jimmy. "We always used to use the manholes."

Jimmy sighed. He was beginning to realize that neither Viggo nor Saffron had any idea how to get inside NJ7. They would never be able to get to the metal door inside Number Ten, Downing Street, because of all the security around it; the tailor's shop could have been any one of hundreds that were in the area. Yannick had been looking around, but really it was a wild goose chase. As for the door under Westminster Bridge, actually in the river, Jimmy was the only one who could breathe underwater. Anyway, Jimmy thought, even if they did get inside, it was only an assumption that his parents were still at NJ7 HQ. He was feeling thoroughly dejected.

Four trains came, four trains left, whisking passengers away and bringing more to fill the platform for a minute or two until they filtered to the exits. All the while, the passageways brought more people to stand and wait—a constant flow of new faces, except for the six who stayed, examining the walls.

"I'm having some chocolate," Felix called out. "Can I borrow fifty pence?" He was standing in front of the snack machine with that familiar look on his face that meant "I need sugar." Viggo felt around in his pockets, irritated at the distraction.

"Do you want anything, Jimmy?" Felix said.

"Yeah, okay." He reasoned that chocolate was always a good decision.

"I'll need a quid, then, Vigs." Felix had already started pushing the buttons to make his selection.

"I haven't got any change. Can't you wait?" said Viggo.

"Come on, just a quid, Viggy," said Felix. Jimmy laughed.

"Honestly, I don't have any. You can't rescue anybody with change in your pockets."

Felix was pressing buttons frantically now, as if he might find the right combination to unlock the delights within. Eva and Georgie gathered round him, also craving a snack. Nobody had any change.

"It's no good Felix," said Georgie. "There's no magic formula for getting chocolate out of one of those when you haven't got any money."

"It's worth a try, though, isn't it? What happens when one of the train drivers gets hungry? Don't they have a secret code or something?"

"They have sandwiches. And even if there is a secret code,

you're not going to find it by pressing buttons at random."

Felix didn't like the discouragement. His face took on an expression of doubled determination. He started pressing with all his fingers, his tongue hanging out of his mouth. Then . . .

Click!

Felix pulled back from the machine. They had all heard the noise, and turned to look at him. A couple of the passengers waiting for a train had heard it too. A man in a pin-striped suit moved closer. Felix reached into the compartment at the bottom with a look of disbelief on his face. He felt around. No free chocolate. His face fell. But they had all heard something.

"What buttons did you press, Felix?" asked Jimmy.

"I can't remember. But it doesn't matter. I still don't have any chocolate."

In frustration he jerked his foot at the base of the machine. It was hardly a kick—more of a tap—but it was enough. Slowly, as if they were imagining it, the whole snack machine came away from the wall. It hinged open just a crack. Warily they all approached the sliver of black that had appeared, separating the machine from the tiles. A waft of dust puffed up out of the opening and floated to the ceiling.

"Wow! Think how much chocolate must be behind there!" Felix exclaimed.

"Oh, don't be an idiot. That's the tunnel," said Eva.

"Quick," said Viggo, snapping into action.

He reached his fingers round the side of the machine and heaved the whole thing open like a chocolate-filled door. Just a small opening was enough. Viggo guided them one by one through this strange porthole. Saffron went first to make sure it was safe, then silently beckoned to the others. Nobody spoke.

Finally, Viggo stepped through himself and pulled the gateway shut behind him. They were standing in the dark. Confused, the man in the pin-striped suit started tapping away at the chocolate machine.

"Stand still while your eyes adjust," said Viggo. "There should be some electric lights in here somewhere."

"I'm still hungry," said Felix.

"Shut up, will you?" Georgie scolded, but then she choked on the thick dust that filled the air.

Gradually, Jimmy started to discern the outlines of the others. It wasn't pitch-black. Slowly, everything was becoming clearer for him. He could see Viggo's face, with his eyes scrunched up. He could see the grime coating the walls, the wires that ran higgledy-piggledy all over the place, and now the people he was with.

"Damn," whispered Viggo. "No lights."

Jimmy looked at Viggo and saw his face still all screwed up, squinting. "I can see fine," he said.

"Is that you, Jimmy?"

"Of course it's me." He waved at Viggo. "You're looking straight at me; can't you see me?"

"No, but don't worry. We'll feel our way."

"But there's plenty of light. What are you on about?" Jimmy looked around at everyone; they all had their faces screwed up and their hands stretched out in front of them, feeling for something that wasn't there.

Then the truth dawned. He was the only one who could see. That meant only one thing: his programming had developed the ability to see in the dark. Then he noticed that everything he was seeing had a strange blue haze. It's like night-vision goggles, he thought, except he was seeing in blue, not green.

"It's okay, I've got, er"—Jimmy felt silly saying it—"I've got night vision."

"What?" shrieked Felix, "You can see in this?"

"Yeah, I guess."

"That's so cool. How many fingers am I holding up?" Felix's gesture was far from polite.

"Felix, don't do that."

"Oh, my God—you really can see in the dark!"

The tunnel stretched so far in a straight line that even if it had been brightly lit along the whole length, it would have been impossible to see the end. There was all sorts of debris covering the old tram tracks: bits of twisted metal, wire mesh, broken tiles, glass, and every few steps a puddle. The walls were crumbling too, and all along the dilapidated bricks there were flecks of something that looked like turquoise paint.

"Jimmy, come here," ordered Viggo. "Help everyone into single file behind me, then put my hands on your shoulders." They shuffled along, with Jimmy the eyes of the snake. He could hear Viggo's breathing. Then a noise grew out of the walls—the almost deafening rumble of a train. It sounded so close that Jimmy thought it would burst through the walls of the tunnel. It was as if the train was all around them, but ghostly and invisible. A shower of dust came down on top of them.

When the train had passed, Viggo whispered, "Jimmy, can you see lights on the walls?"

"Yeah. There are bare bulbs. Can't see a switch, though."

"Why have they disconnected them?" Viggo said to himself.

"Why were there lights in here in the first place?" Jimmy asked. "It's abandoned, isn't it?"

"In the early days," Viggo replied, "NJ7 used this tunnel for experiments."

"Experiments? What sort of experiments?" He thought Viggo wasn't going to answer, but then came the slow response.

"Military technology." The hair on Jimmy's neck prickled. He knew what Viggo was implying.

"Jimmy, this is where they tested the technology that's inside you."

Jimmy looked around at the deathly corridor. Then he realized what the flecks of turquoise paint were. In normal light, it would have been obvious: green stripes.

After walking for what seemed like hours, they finally approached the end of the tunnel. Now Jimmy could make out a new noise. It was a high-pitched hiss, combined with a constant *plop* that resonated up and down the tunnel.

"What's that!" shrieked Eva. "Is that a snake?"

"No," Jimmy shouted. "How would a snake get in here?"

"Maybe it was after some chocolate," Felix quipped.

As they neared the end of the tunnel, the noise grew louder. Now Jimmy knew perfectly well what it was. He could see where it was coming from.

"I think I know why NJ7 stopped doing experiments in this tunnel."

"I think I just realized that too, Jimmy."

WELCOME BACK

Jimmy looked round at Viggo. A trickle of filthy water was tracing a line through the muck on his face. Ahead of them, the Thames was impatiently forcing its way through the wall of the tunnel. A high-pressure jet of water blasted out at them, making a ghastly noise like a screaming animal. Jimmy looked around him at the makeshift repairs from long ago. There was water dripping from the ceiling and running down the walls on both sides. In some places the water came down in torrents, with slime growing in the waterfall. Another chunk of ancient brick crumbled away, brushed aside by the jet of water. The stream was growing all the time.

Christopher Viggo left the chain and blindly felt his way along one side wall. His hands pushed through the streams of water, brushing aside the oozing slime.

"Jimmy," he called out, "there has to be a way through this wall. Can you see one?"

"It looks like the rest of the tunnel, except for the water."

Jimmy stepped over to the wall.

"I'm getting wet!" shouted Eva. "Help me, Chris!"

"Shut up, Eva." It was Georgie shouting back this time. "Of course you're wet."

"Jimmy"—it was Viggo—"listen." He was banging the wall with a bit of stray rock. "Can you hear that?"

"What?"

"It's hollow here. They've bricked up an archway."

"Does that mean we're trapped?" Eva sounded genuinely scared.

The spray of water and muck coated them as they stood there in blackness. Jimmy felt a buzzing in his head. It was his programming. Every day it was becoming more sophisticated. Now it felt much more like a part of him.

"Out the way." Jimmy gathered his thoughts and took a deep breath. Then he reached down inside himself and started stirring up whatever he could. He felt strength energizing his muscles. He ran his finger over the gash on his wrist. It hadn't healed, but it didn't need to. It was a reminder to Jimmy of everything about him that wasn't human. He focused on that part of his spirit now. "Time to walk through walls," he said.

Viggo moved to one side and nearly fell over a broken chair. Jimmy stared at the side wall, while to his left, at the very end of the tunnel, the Thames was fighting its way in. He took two bold steps, then jumped. His feet crashed into the wall. With the force of a bulldozer, he split the crumbling brickwork.

It fell away like stale crackers and exposed a stretch of tunnel only about three meters long. It had the same concrete block walls and the same simple lighting as the corridors of NJ7, and at its end was a metal door.

There was brick dust swirling around now, mixing with the muck and the water that was already in the air. The others blinked at the new light.

"Come on!" Jimmy shouted from the top of a pile of rubble.

Eva screamed. The hole Jimmy had bashed in the side wall hadn't settled. Fragments of brick carried on breaking off. But Eva was looking at the wall at the end of the tram tunnel. It was trembling. The vibrations from Jimmy's kick had carried round. The holes where the water was busting through were growing. Amid the mess, Jimmy saw cracks flash like lightning into the wall.

"Get over here!" he roared, but the noise was too much now—the water, the crumbling of the wall, the cracking. They had a matter of seconds to get through the door. Viggo ran ahead and pushed it open. He, like Jimmy, knew that the doors of NJ7 were never locked. They were going to make it. But then . . .

The noise mounted higher and higher. They all felt the rumbling in the floor throbbing up their legs. Another train. This was it. The tunnel would never survive. They rushed through the hole in the wall. One by one they skipped over Jimmy, still lying among the broken bricks: Felix, Georgie, Saffron, all into the corridor and sprinting for the door that Viggo was holding open for them. Only Eva couldn't move. Was it fear that rooted her to the spot? Or was it the tissue in her shoes shrinking, making it impossible for her to walk? The train boomed all around them, unseen, but so close.

Jimmy sprang to his feet. He leaped back through the hole in the wall, into the tunnel. Eva turned from the jets of water to Jimmy, her eyes gushing.

Bang!

The bricks of the wall between the tunnel and the river shot out with the force of cannonballs. Slabs of brick peppered Jimmy's back as he sheltered Eva. He grabbed the terrified girl round her waist. Sweeping her off her feet, Jimmy hit the other side of the tunnel and immediately jumped back. The water was charging in now. With a heavy thud, they landed back in the NJ7 tunnel. The noise was immense, as the Thames found a new hole to devour. It thrashed its way in, gobbling up the debris on the floor.

Jimmy snatched Eva's collar and ran, dragging her behind him. The water was running with them, thirsty for the space they were in. Then they were through the metal door, and Viggo slammed it shut.

"It'll never hold!" shouted Georgie. A pool of putrid liquid surrounded them.

"It's okay; at NJ7 they think of everything," said Viggo, reaching for a discreet button at the side of the door. "It's a flood button. It seals the door."

"Of course," muttered Jimmy. "The doors at threat from flooding must be fitted with these, and then if they want to flood the whole complex, they just release the door."

"One hundred twenty seconds," said Viggo, striding away from them and down the new corridor. "That's all it would take for this whole place to be underwater."

They walked in silence. Jimmy wordlessly took the lead and pressed his memory into action. They moved cautiously as Jimmy tried to pull up something, anything that would tell him the geography of the huge labyrinth they were in. But all the tunnels looked the same—endless avenues of gray concrete blocks.

185

"Come on, Jimmy, think," Saffron whispered behind him.

"Shhh. I am thinking!" he hissed back.

"Wait." It was Viggo's reassuring voice. "Don't think."

"What?"

"Turn off your thoughts. Trust your instinct. You're a machine aren't you?"

"No. I'm thirty-eight percent human," growled Jimmy.

"Well, the rest of you isn't. Machines don't have to think, do they?"

It was just like Dr. Higgins had told Jimmy in training. "Do what your programming tells you, not what you want to do," Dr. Higgins had said.

Jimmy shut his eyes. If only there were a switch he could just flick, he thought, then turning on his programming would be easy. After a couple of seconds he felt that swelling in his belly. But he had to keep enough control over it to stop him from trying to complete his original mission: kill Christopher Viggo.

A swirling gray soup cloaked his head. Here it comes, he thought; just a little more. The muscles up the back of his neck fizzed, then his thoughts stopped coming, held on the cusp of his attention, like a voice you can't quite hear. In their place was a pounding confidence. That feeling reached down through his skull and pulled words up from his throat. At the same time, iron strength pushed his breath up from his middle.

"This way," he announced suddenly, and set off fast, just short of a run.

The tunnel forked in two or hit a junction at regular intervals. Jimmy always turned boldly in the direction his instinct told him to go. He was like a hound following a scent. The others followed without question.

Sooner than anyone realized, they arrived at the room where Dr. Higgins had explained Jimmy's nature. It was the room where he had been briefly reunited with his parents, before Paduk had taken them away again. Here were the computers, here was the old-fashioned wooden desk with nothing on it but a pen, and here were the six technicians.

Here too was Dr. Higgins.

"Jimmy, welcome back," his wiry voice enunciated, without even turning round.

Jimmy pulled his mind out of the fog just before a strange and very strong feeling took him over. It had sprung up at the sound of Dr. Higgins's voice. What was that? Appreciation? Love? Devotion? Jimmy quashed it.

"Take the others. Find my parents," Jimmy whispered at Viggo, who immediately marshaled the rest into order and led them away.

"Good luck, Jimmy," Georgie called out as she turned the corner. Jimmy turned too late to see her face.

"Yes, let the others go." Dr. Higgins sneered. "Paduk's watching. He'll soon pick them up. I want to talk to *you*, Jimmy."

Suddenly Jimmy felt a rush of guilt. What had he done? Viggo, Saffron, Georgie, Eva, and Felix were gone before he could stop them. How could he have brought them into danger like this? He felt so childish for mistrusting Viggo.

Jimmy edged round the desk. He kept his eyes on Dr. Higgins and watched his face, more manic than ever.

"Tell me, Jimmy," he seethed, "did your training work? Did it take control?"

Jimmy's throat was blocked again. Then he choked out, "Yes, it did."

"You'll have to speak up, Jimmy; I really am a little deaf, you know." Dr. Higgins smiled a yellow smile.

"It did. My training took control."

"But Viggo isn't dead. Yet. Miss Bennett was most upset when she heard. She suggested killing you. Still, you've done well to lead him here. Tell me, why didn't you kill Viggo?"

"I didn't want to."

"You didn't *want* to?" Dr. Higgins paused. "But your programming, your mission . . . ?"

"I want to get rid of it," Jimmy announced proudly. "I don't want to work for NJ7 and I want to leave with my parents."

"Of course, you're only eleven—the training isn't complete." Dr. Higgins nodded and stroked his chin. "The assassin in you is not yet powerful enough. If only the other one . . . But you wait; when you're eighteen, there'll be no stopping you." He lifted his face and winked at Jimmy. It sent a shiver down his spine.

"I don't want it. You have to deprogram me, or whatever."

"Was it exciting, Jimmy?"

"Did you hear me?" Jimmy shouted. "I want to get rid of it."

"Oh, you can't do that, Jimmy. You're only thirty-eight percent human, and without the cellular mechanics, I'm afraid you would die." Dr. Higgins sounded genuinely disappointed when he said that. "Now tell me"—his face lightened again—"how did you try to kill Christopher Viggo? Did you try to blow him up? Or you stabbed him in the back, didn't you? Or perhaps you took the most fashionable option and injected him with a deadly virus? I told you: just a single blow to the neck,

Jimmy. You were more creative, though, weren't you?"

Jimmy shuddered. "We fenced," he said.

"What?"

"We fenced. You know, sword fighting," said Jimmy. "That's how I fought with Christopher Viggo. With skewers."

"Fencing with skewers? That isn't part of your training." Dr. Higgins was squeezing his pen so hard that Jimmy was sure it would snap. "Sword fighting hasn't been part of a secret agent's repertoire for centuries."

Jimmy dropped his eyes to the floor. "Well, that's what we did," he mumbled. His mind was racing. If that hadn't been part of his programming . . .

Dr. Higgins was furious. He threw his chair back and stormed round the room. The veins in his neck were bulging out from the top of his white coat.

"That's outrageous!" he ranted. "You must listen to your programming!"

"I *was* listening," Jimmy shouted back. "And it nearly worked, but now I don't want it. I am not a killer. Reprogram me! Make me into a robot that doesn't kill!"

At those words the room burst out laughing. Even the technicians were shaking their heads, suddenly full of good humor.

"I'm afraid we can't do that, Jimmy." Dr. Higgins's veins were fading back to the gray of his skin. "You're not as simple as a computer. It's woven into your DNA. It's the way you are. And that's the way you are always going to be." He let a smile escape onto his mouth. "It can only get stronger."

Jimmy wanted to object, but he could feel instinctively that it was all true. That pool behind his stomach bubbled away, as if his own insides were mocking him.

189

"I'm not a computer, I'm not a robot, and I'm not human," Jimmy cried. Then he screamed in horror, "What am I?"

"Like the rest of us," Dr. Higgins soberly pronounced, "you are the sum of your actions. And your actions, Jimmy, are dictated by what you are—and you are a killer. Now, come back and kill for us, Jimmy. We're the good guys."

Jimmy was quaking with anger and confusion. "Where are my parents?"

"You can see them when you agree to return to us." Dr. Higgins sat back in his comfortable chair, swaying from side to side, his pen held playfully in his fingers. His fingers looked thinner than the pen. "Miss Bennett and Paduk . . ." He paused, looking for the right words. "They can be much more persuasive."

"You can't torture me."

"Ha! Of course we can't. You're designed to withstand any torture. *Physical* torture, that is."

"What do you mean?"

"I mean that there are three members of the Coates family currently in NJ7 HQ, and none of them is quite as resilient as you in the face of pain."

Jimmy's anger washed through him like a flood. With it came the killing instinct he hated. He was about to pounce, but as his weight shifted he caught movement in his peripheral vision. The technicians weren't going to let him get near Dr. Higgins. Two of them sprang out of their chairs, one on each side. It appeared they were trained in more than just computer skills.

Jimmy jumped straight up into the air. As the technicians came at him, he stretched his legs out and spun round, kicking them both in the face simultaneously. They fell back, giving Jimmy just enough time to land and leap onto the desk. He grabbed Dr. Higgins by the throat, pushing the man back in his chair. The force sent the chair toppling backward, and Jimmy landed with a knee on either side of Dr. Higgins's chest. Then he snatched the pen from Dr. Higgins's bony fingers. The technicians were rushing forward, but Dr. Higgins held up a hand to stop them.

"It's okay," he hissed, right into Jimmy's face.

Jimmy held the pen in his fist, digging the point into the side of Dr. Higgins's neck. The old man's face was unflinching. He hadn't even blinked.

"Kill me, Jimmy," he whispered. "Go on. I'm an old man. I'd be glad to go like this: dying for my country. Kill me."

Jimmy stared into the rusty eyes of his old next-door neighbor.

"Come on!" Dr. Higgins shouted, his mouth only centimeters from Jimmy's, spittle dancing on his lips. Jimmy pushed the pen a little harder. Dr. Higgins winced with the pain for the first time. "What are you waiting for? You're a killer—kill me!" But then his shout disintegrated into a raucous laugh. His veins bulged red and purple again. Jimmy was panting, flustered. What was happening? He didn't want to kill anybody, but his programming did, and it had swamped him, seizing control. So why was he hesitating?

"You can't kill me." Dr. Higgins sneered. "A little something I slipped into the programming." Jimmy loosened his fist round the pen, and it dropped to the floor. "Do you see, Jimmy? You *have* to work for me. Because you can't kill me."

Jimmy rolled off the doctor and scrambled to his feet,

dusting his knees to hide the fact that his hands were quivering. Dr. Higgins was helped up by one of the technicians. The other five floated around, desperate to get between Jimmy and Dr. Higgins. Two of them stepped forward, muscles tense, ready for aggressive action. They didn't realize Jimmy's objective was to get as far away from the doctor as possible.

He glared for a moment into the old man's eyes, then spun round and bolted up the passage. He had to find the others before they found trouble.

20

FINAL OFFER

"Don't these tunnels *lead* anywhere?" cried Felix, exasperated.

"I'm sure we've passed that metal door before," said Eva quietly, so that only Georgie could hear. She didn't want to upset Viggo anymore. He had already glared at her when she had been moaning.

"No, it's just a different door," Georgie whispered back. "It must be." She didn't sound convinced. The more she thought about it, in fact, the more she felt like they had just been going round in circles. There had certainly been no sign of her parents.

"Are you sure they're here, Chris?" asked Saffron.

"Of course they're here," said Viggo. "They're still agents."

"But they're agents being held prisoner."

"I know, but . . ." He turned—and froze. Looking along the line, he saw the expectant expressions of Saffron, Felix, Georgie, and Eva. And behind Eva loomed the huge frame of Paduk. Eva hadn't even noticed. He beamed a cheesy smile at

Viggo, and his green stripe boasted proudly on his uniform. How long had he been following them?

"What's the matter?" said Saffron.

Viggo didn't answer. Instead he charged at Paduk, roughly shoving the others out of his way. They bounced off the walls of the narrow corridor. The smile on Paduk's face turned to a look of concentration, and he cracked his jaw.

As Viggo surged past, Eva screamed. Paduk's arm snapped up from his side. A revolver was leveled straight at Viggo's head. Paduk took a second to aim, but a second was too long. Viggo was on him, forcing the gun out of Paduk's fist.

Bang!

The gun went off just above Eva's head. Her hands clapped over her ears. The bullet ricocheted off the side of the tunnel as the gun hit the floor. Before Saffron could move for it, a weight hit her side with the force of a rocket. Doubled up, she turned to see a line of agents waiting to take her on, one by one. They were surrounded.

Eva stayed on the floor clutching her ears, but Georgie threw herself on top of Paduk, who was on the floor, wrestling with Viggo.

Felix ran toward Saffron, pelting into an NJ7 agent like an incensed ram. He hurled low-level jabs and even tried biting, but Saffron gave him a disapproving look. Her own hand-to-hand combat was as good as her driving. She mixed martial arts and boxing with amazing athleticism.

Gradually, the fight drifted down the corridor in the direction of the metal door. Paduk and Viggo were constantly chasing after Paduk's gun, pounding each other against the wall of the tunnel, while Saffron was backing up. Between the two fights, the dazed and deafened Eva crawled away, terrified.

Paduk swung at Georgie with one hand and Viggo with the other. His eyes were sharp and mean. Sweat trickled down the side of his cheek, oozing into his collar. Viggo was his warped mirror image. His suit was more crumpled and his looks more swarthy, but his fighting was just as acute. In the corner of his eye, he saw a huge fist come flying toward Georgie. . . .

But Viggo was there. He ducked into the punch, taking its force himself, then staggered back onto Georgie. Paduk took his chance. He spun round and scooped up his gun. When he turned back, Viggo was on the floor, just waiting to be shot.

"I'll take the kid alive." Paduk sneered with glee. "But you they want dead." He glared into Viggo's eyes and took aim. His finger squeezed the trigger. Georgie screamed; Eva screamed; Felix screamed, even though he hadn't seen what was happening.

Dooiinngg!

Viggo winced — but that wasn't the sound of a gun going off, and that didn't feel like a bullet penetrating his skull. The ringing of metal echoed over the grunts of the agents still fighting Saffron. A shadow filled the space behind Paduk. Then Paduk fell forward, slowly. His eyes were still full of the anger that comes with killing, but now they were glazed over. As his jaw gave one last click, he slumped on top of Viggo. Standing over him was Yannick, brandishing a frying pan.

Viggo shrugged off Paduk's giant body and embraced the chef. But Yannick pushed him away and raised the frying pan above his head.

"Duck!" he shouted, flinging the frying pan down the corridor.

Saffron dropped to the ground. Felix wasn't so fast, but fortunately, the huge iron pan passed over his head. It clunked into the chest of an approaching NJ7 agent. He crumpled back into the arms of the one agent who was still standing. In that split second, Viggo snatched up Georgie and bundled Yannick out of the metal door he had come in by. Felix and Saffron dragged Eva toward the exit. Then they heard a determined scream.

"Go! Go!" Jimmy was hurtling toward them at top speed. "Get out of here. Now!" Jimmy's voice throbbed with authority. They dove through the door just as the crack of the last agent's gun hit their ears. Jimmy was coming so fast he was a blur. Then there was a muffled *splat*, and Jimmy fell to the ground.

"Meet me with transport outside Number Ten, Downing Street," he cried, struggling to his feet.

"What transport?" Saffron replied as the door swung closed between them.

"Something fast." And with that, the metal door slammed shut. Saffron found herself staring into a full-length tailor's mirror.

Alarms bled into the silence. Then Yannick spluttered into action.

"It took me ages to work out which mirror it was."

"What?" said Viggo.

"This is the tailor's shop you told me to look for. I broke in."

"But how did you know it was this one?"

"It's the Savoy Tailors' Guild. We're next door to the Savoy." He said it as if it were obvious. Viggo's expression made an actual question superfluous, so Yannick carried on. "I remembered from the time I was working at the Savoy, more people came in here than went out. Tonight I realized this must be the place."

"So how come I didn't know about it?" Viggo was suddenly grumpy.

"You must have resigned before they set it up."

They moved through the shop in dreamlike disbelief.

Yannick fingered the shirts with appreciation. "Hold on. I'll just see if they have an eighteen-inch collar."

"That's shoplifting; you'll get arrested!" Georgie shouted above the wail of the alarm.

Yannick looked slightly irritated. "Let me see," he said, piling shirts into his arms. "I've broken into the headquarters of the secret police, we're planning to kidnap two of the prime minister's agents, and I'm aiding the escape of public enemy number one."

"Okay," Georgie mumbled. "But shoplifting is still wrong."

She didn't really care what Yannick did to the contents of the shop. In her mind she was running over what had happened as they escaped from the tunnel.

"Jimmy wasn't . . ." She hesitated, looking over the others' faces. "He wasn't . . . *shot*, was he?"

There was no answer. The ringing of the alarm bells intensified in her ears. She didn't notice the scores of people pointing at them as they all filed out of the tailor's shop. Police sirens screamed louder.

"Let's get out of here," Viggo said, flatly.

Jimmy made short work of the one NJ7 agent left in the corridor. He could hear the steps of others pattering toward him, but there was no chance of anyone stopping him. It was as if the rest of the world moved in slow motion. His body twisted and flipped so fast, his opponent had no idea how to react. But for Jimmy, it was only as if he was stretching after a long night's sleep.

The only thing tense about him was his left fist. He turned his arm round. There was his wrist with that familiar gash. He opened his palm. A bullet lay there like a steel jellybean.

Slipping it into his pocket, he ran, knowing exactly where to go. The tunnels of NJ7 held no mysteries for him now, even if his own body did. Power surged through him, his senses battering him with information about the tiniest details, yet his brain was fast enough to process all of it. It was as if the air he breathed was fresh from a tropical island, after years in a cardboard box. Something in him had been released.

He sprinted on with one aim in mind, brushing aside anyone who tried to get in his way. In no time at all he was there: a small metal door distinguishable from the others only by the untidy addition of the number ten. He burst through it, never more determined to take his parents to safety, never more sure that he was going to succeed.

"Jimmy, welcome once again." The wiry voice of the prime minister matched his withered appearance. "I hope the trouble you are causing will be swiftly resolved."

"Give me my parents," Jimmy said, sounding as calm as Viggo might have done.

"Your parents are waiting just in here." Ares Hollingdale stretched out an arm extravagantly. It looked as if he were faintly amused by the grit in Jimmy's expression. They walked together through rooms that Jimmy remembered only too well, and found themselves back in that perfect reception room. Flowery wallpaper encased them, and the too-soft sofas stood like sentries round the fireplace. In their arms they held Ian and Helen Coates. Jimmy let his face relax into the biggest smile he had ever felt. But they were not smiling back.

His parents were balancing cups of tea in their hands, the fine porcelain saucers and wafer-thin teacups rattling with their obvious concern.

"I do hope you have come to tell me you are still working for me, Jimmy." There was a hint of tiredness in the prime minister's voice. "Otherwise I shall have to kill these two people, whom you have known as your parents for so long." He brushed a hand in their direction almost regally. "That would be a shame because I believe that they are still good agents, and could be valuable to this country."

Jimmy knew he could easily snap the prime minister in two, but that would be giving up control to the killer inside him. I'm not an assassin, he kept telling himself. I'm not here to kill the prime minister.

"I haven't yet decided whether or not you will have to be disposed of yourself." Hollingdale narrowed his eyes to slits and aimed them at the space between Jimmy's eyebrows. "You were very expensive. Dr. Higgins is keen that you be allowed another seven years to develop. Miss Bennett, however, is of the view that if you've gone this wrong so soon, it would be best to prevent you from becoming a bigger problem."

Even after everything that had happened, Jimmy had some shock left in his system: his teacher wanted to "dispose" of him. Still, he didn't say a word, fearing what might come out if he opened his mouth. He didn't look at his parents either. The sight of them sitting obediently in their places, scared for their lives, might have sent his programming into overdrive. He didn't want to lose control.

"So what's it to be, young man?" Hollingdale said, before sipping at his tea with a vulgar slurping noise. There was a long silence, colored only by a distant agitation coming from somewhere outside the building. Jimmy didn't want to say anything. Surely they knew what the answer was going to be? His parents at least must have been aware that Jimmy would never agree to work as an assassin. They were offering no reaction though. At last, Hollingdale broke the stalemate.

"Jimmy," he started, trying to soften his voice, but failing, "you could help me do away with lots and lots of nasty people." He sounded like he was reading a children's story now, but one that was too young for Jimmy. "You have a choice to make between the deaths of your parents, two charming and talented people, and the deaths of the criminal element of society. Work with me, Jimmy, and you could live happily as a family again."

He rose from his chair, as if to catch up with his voice. "Together, you and I could sweep away all the democratic terrorists who want to waste time on changing governments every five years. When this country needs action, we can't afford to dither and debate. Just think, in only a few years, we could do away completely with the overweight, the lazy, and the French!"

Jimmy looked across at his parents for the first time. His mother was gazing at him imploringly, tears gathering in her eyes. His father was staring into his tea. What was he thinking? The prime minister walked over to the fireplace and paused for breath.

Just then the door wafted open gently, rubbing against the thick carpet. In walked the one person Jimmy didn't want to see.

Miss Bennett had a smile curling all the way up one side of her face. Her eyelashes seemed to scroll up endlessly, like the claws of a deadly insect. She spoke without taking her eyes off Jimmy.

"Prime Minister . . ."

"Hush, dear, I want his answer."

"But Prime Minister—"

He turned sharply, infuriated. "Can't you see he's about to give me his answer?"

"I'm afraid Christopher Viggo has already given us his answer." The prime minister's face fell. The bags under his eyes seemed to deepen and the lines on his face cut deeper. It was only then that Jimmy realized what he could hear. Outside there were sirens, shouts, and gunshots. Then he made out the distinctive moan of helicopter blades—Viggo had found transport.

Hollingdale turned back to Jimmy, looking as if his best friend had just betrayed him.

"Which means," announced Miss Bennett in a girlie singsong, "that it is time to kill all three of you." She padded across the carpet, her patterned shoes sinking a centimeter with each step.

"But, do you really think . . . ?"

"I'm afraid so, Prime Minister. This is one investment that has gone rotten."

Jimmy's head was spinning. His parents were still sitting there, motionless. Were they just waiting to die? If they were

NJ7 agents, why didn't they get up and fight? Then he thought of Viggo and Saffron. They were on their way to rescue him. Any second now, and they would have fought their way into the building. Outside the gunshots pounded away; the shouting intensified.

"They're not coming for you, Jimmy," Miss Bennett said, reading his mind from his desperate glance toward the window. "In a couple of minutes, they will all be dead. Including that annoying girl who keeps screaming, our mutual friend Felix— shame about him, but never mind—and of course"—she paused, savoring her delight, and licked her lips—"your sister."

At those words, Jimmy felt something in him click. Suddenly, everything in his head shifted to one side, and every-thing in his body jumped the other way. Now they were in line. His heart pounded and his head responded. In the corridors of NJ7 he had felt in tune with his programming, but now he felt that he *was* his programming. For the first time, there was a single, unified mind in operation. He was all just Jimmy Coates.

He looked over to Miss Bennett. Her expression told him she knew she had made a mistake. Her hands moved smoothly to the holster on her thigh, but Jimmy was quicker. He jumped onto the back of one of the sofas and leaped at his teacher. The sofa toppled backward, and as it hit the floor, Jimmy kicked Miss Bennett's gun out of her hands. It bounced against the wall, and a bullet pinged into the portrait of Tony Blair. It left a hole where one of his teeth should have been.

Jimmy swept his foot across Miss Bennett's knees, bringing her down. As she fell, her head hit the door handle. She slumped in a still-glamorous pile, unconscious.

"Don't do this, Jimmy," shouted the prime minister. "You'll never get away!"

Jimmy glanced up and saw fear in his sallow complexion.

"The sound of that gun will bring my bodyguards here in a flash."

"If they even heard it," Jimmy replied calmly. "I think they're all busy." Indeed, the noise of the battle outside had escalated. Nobody could have made out the sound of one more bullet. Jimmy took a step toward Hollingdale.

"Jimmy," started his father, leaping to his feet at last, "don't do anything rash. He's the prime minister."

"He's a maniac," Jimmy shouted back. Don't start telling me off now, he thought.

"That's right, Jimmy," said Hollingdale, backing into the fireplace, "don't do anything you'll regret. Let's keep this civilized."

"I'm not going to kill you," Jimmy said through his teeth, "because I'm not a killer." In a flash, he dove back to the center of the room and rolled over onto his feet. As soon as he was upright, he snatched two teacups from the coffee table. His wrists flicked with the force of a crossbow, and he sent two saucers spinning in opposite directions. Tea splashed over the middle of the room. One saucer whizzed toward the window and shattered it. The other, spinning remorselessly, cracked into the middle of Ares Hollingdale's chest. It split in two and dropped to the carpet.

The old man stood absolutely still for a long time, then tottered three steps to his left, and collapsed.

"Let's go," shouted Jimmy, making for the window. The noise of gunfire from the street was fierce now. The police had brought in machine guns, and still the helicopter roared.

Jimmy's mother made to follow him, then suddenly stopped. Ian Coates was not following them. Jimmy turned at the threshold of the room and saw his father standing over the unconscious body of the prime minister.

"Let's go!" Jimmy shouted again, the gusts from the helicopter sending his hair in chaotic spirals.

"You had a job to do, Jimmy." Ian Coates's voice was hard, but with the quiver of emotion. "A job for your country. And for your parents."

Jimmy couldn't believe what he was hearing.

"Don't do this to me again, Ian," said Jimmy's mother.

"We have to go now!" Jimmy shouted. Through the window he could see armed police advancing on the helicopter, which hovered only meters from the paving stones. He could see Viggo at the controls. Saffron was scattering bullets into the crowd of attackers. Jimmy's father spoke as if there was nothing happening in the street outside, as if the only battle was in that very room. Prime ministers from the past stared down at them sternly. Two bodies spoiled the pattern on the carpet.

"Helen, I'm not coming with you," he said. "I have a duty to my country, and my prime minister."

"The prime minister is mad, Ian; he's evil." A tear glistened on the precipice of Helen Coates's eye. "We knew it thirteen years ago, and it's been driving us apart ever since. You have to come with me. You won't make me stay. It's not like last time."

Jimmy felt his confusion wrenching apart everything inside him.

"Mum, what's going on?" he whimpered. "What do you mean, 'last time'?"

His mother turned to him. The tears were etching lines across her cheeks now, blown in all directions by the wind coming through the broken window. "Jimmy, I wanted to leave NJ7 thirteen years ago. But your father didn't."

"So why didn't you?"

"Yes, why didn't you, Helen?" said Ian Coates, looking up at his wife with a yearning in his eyes.

"You know why," was Helen's soft reply. "Because I loved you. But this time I have to go." She turned away from him and stepped up to the window, where Jimmy was waiting. She didn't look back.

"No, Dad!" Jimmy shouted. There were tears in his eyes now too, but it could have been from the swirling wind; it blew spiteful dust into his face. "Dad! Come with us! Come on!"

"Get out of here!" his father shouted back. "Get out before I raise the alarm."

"No! I came to rescue you!" Jimmy longed for the world to stop.

Ian Coates turned away.

"I'll let you go, but I'm not coming with you," he said without looking up.

For a moment, Jimmy lost all the strength he had. He looked back at his mother. She was already climbing over the splintered glass. Jimmy had to move, but as he did, something inside his head was screaming. The last thing he saw as he jumped out of the window was his father kneeling down to place a cushion behind the prime minister's head.

21

EXILE

The street was in total disorder. Hundreds of police were shouting, running about, and firing any weapon they could find. The army had arrived with heavier guns, and even a ground-to-air missile. Everyone was trying to bring down the helicopter and the people inside it. Viggo was a skilled pilot, though, trained in evasion and the art of staying in the air.

The breaking of the prime minister's window had hardly registered in most people's minds. The few who had noticed it thought it must have been just more damage from a stray bullet, or from the bits of debris blown around by the force of the helicopter. Nobody noticed an eleven-year-old killing machine and his mother climbing into the street.

Nobody except Felix.

"There he is!" he shouted, although there was no way he could be heard. Inside the helicopter they were all wearing earphones to protect them from the massive din. Viggo and Saffron were both wearing helmets.

The helicopter was larger than the one Jimmy had flown, with a row of benches lining either side of its belly. Felix, Eva, Georgie, and Yannick were strapped in there. Viggo handled the controls, taking the machine up, down, and around with immense facility. It was hardly still for a moment. Meanwhile, Saffron sent rounds of ammunition into the armed forces below.

"There's Jimmy and his mum!" Felix screamed again. Viggo followed Felix's frantic pointing. He saw two figures, hunched against the wind, making their way through the distracted military guard.

Felix watched Viggo's face change. For a moment it showed a softness. As if he had seen something that he had lost long ago—something he thought he would never see again. Then the steel returned behind his eyes, and he gave Felix a firm thumbs-up.

"Time to get this baby going," he said.

Felix grinned toothily at Eva and Georgie as the chopper staggered higher, out of range of the guns below. Then it turned to face them head-on.

Jimmy saw the figures of his friends grow smaller. He stopped running.

"Wait," he said, holding a hand out in front of his mother. He looked around. Hundreds of people who all had instructions to kill him were staring up at the sky, unaware that their principal target was among them, unchallenged.

Then the helicopter started its descent, swooping like a bird of prey. Jimmy knew exactly what Viggo was going to do. It's what he would have done. The rockets on the side of the helicopter fired up. In a flash, they surged ahead.

"Keep your eyes on the helicopter," Jimmy shouted to his mother, "and whatever happens, run toward it."

Helen Coates nodded. Her expression was serene. "I've done this more times than you think."

There was no time to be shocked by his mother's reply, but it wasn't what he was expecting.

This time the rockets caused considerably more damage than when Jimmy had fired into the Thames. The old stones of the London street weren't built to withstand missile attacks at close range. Even the reinforced gates at the entrance to Downing Street were blasted out of all recognition. Dust clouds billowed into the air, cutting out all the light. Beneath the boom of the dual explosion was the screaming of officers, blown into the air.

Jimmy and Helen Coates clung to each other. They were blown off their feet, but the missiles had hit far enough away for them to be among the first to recover. Behind them, the windows of Downing Street cried shards of their ancient glass. After a second to steady themselves, Jimmy and his mother ran toward the shadow emerging from the soot.

Blowing itself a clearance through the blackness, the helicopter swept down as low as it could in the narrow street. Some of the lampposts had been bent out of shape by the blast, so Viggo could fly lower than he had expected. Saffron was ready with a rope, nonetheless. It dropped to the street just a few meters in front of Jimmy. The sight of it was such a relief that when Jimmy jumped and attached himself to it he felt he never wanted to let go. Immediately he started pulling himself up. One glance down told him his mother had also safely caught the rope. She was climbing as fast as Jimmy, who was amazed at her agility.

The clouds of dust obscured the view of the soldiers in the street. Even those who were upright again, and had found their guns, had nothing to aim at. By the time their view cleared, their enemy was nowhere to be seen. With two new passengers, the helicopter soared away into the night.

Georgie was the first out of her seat. She leaped up and threw her arms round her brother.

"Oh, Jimmy! I thought you'd been shot!"

"I nearly was," he said, his lungs constricted by the tight squeeze. Pulling himself away, he slipped his hand into his pocket and presented his sister with the bullet.

"Thanks for coming to get us," Jimmy said, turning to Viggo, who was still focused on being the pilot.

"Mission accomplished," Viggo shouted, without looking back.

Jimmy felt a heaviness inside him, and knew why only too well. He had escaped from NJ7 with only half of what he came for: his mother, but not his father.

"Where's Dad?" Georgie shouted, swamped in her mother's hug. There was no answer. Helen looked across at the back of Viggo's head, then buried her face in her daughter's hair.

"Did you find *my* parents, Jimmy?" Felix had a smile on his face that Jimmy could easily see was forced. Jimmy solemnly shook his head.

"Your parents are heroes," said Saffron, sitting next to Felix and putting an arm round him, "and they'd be proud of you."

Felix hunched his shoulders, uncomfortable in Saffron's protective squeeze.

"Don't say it like they're dead," he huffed, but Saffron

was quick to reassure him.

"Of course they're not dead—you're keeping them alive."

"What?" Felix surveyed the faces of everyone in the helicopter, as Saffron continued.

"While Jimmy hides, NJ7 may never find him. But they know he's with you, and they know the one thing that will bring Jimmy out of hiding might be trying to rescue your parents. My guess is that Hollingdale will not only make sure your parents stay alive, but he'll somehow make it very obvious where he's holding them."

"So you're saying my mum and dad are bait for Jimmy?"

"For Chris too, I suppose. And bait is useless if it's dead."

Felix considered what he had heard.

"Will NJ7 . . . torture them?" he croaked.

"What would be the point?" Saffron responded immediately. "They don't have any secrets to reveal."

Jimmy watched as the tension in Felix's face eased. "We'll find them, don't worry," he called out, as strongly as he could manage. But in his heart he knew it would take time.

Eva shuffled along the bench to be next to Felix.

"You miss them, don't you?" she murmured, so that only Felix could hear. There was no answer. "I miss mine." Felix looked up and saw the sadness in Eva's eyes. "Do you think when we grow up," she said, trembling, "that whatever we do, we can't help becoming like our parents?"

They were soon out of London, clipping along at quite a pace. Viggo brought the helicopter down low over a field somewhere to the south. They carried on zooming through the countryside, low enough to smell the cows.

"Below radar," Saffron explained when Felix asked. "We have to stay at this altitude until they call off the aerial search. Then we'll head somewhere safe." Sure enough, while they waited, army helicopters and fighter jets pounded the sky above them.

"Can't we land?" Yannick moaned, looking increasingly pallid the sicker he became. Viggo ignored him, and held the helicopter hovering barely a meter above the ground, hidden by a clump of trees.

"Hello, Mrs. Coates, I'm Saffron Walden," cooed Saffron, as gently as she could above the noise of the machine they were sitting in.

"Pleased to meet you. And thank you for coming to our rescue." Helen threw a casual look at Viggo. "All of you." Viggo glanced round and held her gaze for a second, then turned away.

"Where did you get the helicopter?" Jimmy asked, to break the awkward silence. It was Georgie who answered.

"It was amazing; we went to the French embassy and just flew it out!"

Saffron explained. "They took one look at Chris in his NJ7 suit and did anything he told them. They're quite used to being ordered about by agents of the Green Stripe." Jimmy was still confused. The French embassy wasn't the first place he would have gone looking for fast transport. Smashing the window of a Ferrari showroom would have been easier.

"What were they doing with a military helicopter at the French embassy?" Jimmy shouted as loud as he could.

"After Hollingdale had the French ambassador sent back to France"—Jimmy remembered the Bentley—"they started taking precautions." Viggo chuckled as he sent the helicopter on a wave of plummets and sudden ascents through the hills. "They have a few high-level military items hidden away in their embassy compound, so I just, well, confiscated this one."

At this, they all burst out laughing. Even Yannick chortled before groaning again and closing his eyes.

"He stole their car, and now he's stolen their helicopter!" Felix roared.

Viggo was taking the engine to new speeds. He pulled out of a dive that took them within spitting distance of a farmhouse, and whisked the rotors up into the clouds.

"Time to get going," he said.

"Where?" said Jimmy, suddenly serious again.

"We'll return this thing to its rightful owners."

"The French embassy?"

"No, the French."

They flew steadily and high enough so that they didn't attract too much attention. It wasn't hard to be invisible in the night sky, and before long they were over water. Jimmy relaxed slightly. The battles of the past few days were over. The country that now meant only danger for him was being left behind. But so was his father.

He took the seat next to Georgie.

"I have to tell you something," he said over the noise, "about Mum and Dad, and about me."

"It's okay, Jimmy," she shouted back. "Mum explained."

"So, you know?"

"Yeah. It's cool. Well, some of it is, anyway." She let a nervous smile soften her lips.

"I suppose it means I'm not your brother."

"Oh, Jimmy." Georgie sighed as the smile took over completely. "Of course you're my brother." Then she hugged him longer and harder than she ever had.

Miss Bennett adjusted the bandage round her head and looked from Dr. Higgins to Paduk, also heavily bandaged.

"Where are they?" she barked, from behind her desk.

"We think they're heading for France," replied Paduk, "but they're avoiding radar, and we can't enter French airspace without causing a major incident."

"Paduk, this *is* a major incident."

She was about to go on, but a tall, slim shadow had appeared in the entrance to her office. Miss Bennett, Paduk, and Dr. Higgins all jumped to attention.

"I haven't been down in these tunnels," intoned the prime minister, "for I don't know how long." Ares Hollingdale stepped slowly in, admiring Miss Bennett's efforts at decorating the harsh NJ7 room. On the walls were postcards showing some of Stubbs's finest paintings of horses, but these were overshadowed by the massive Union Jack that hung behind Miss Bennett's desk. The red and blue were rich and gleaming, but right in the center of the flag, standing out like a bonfire, was a bold green stripe.

"What are we going to do about this?" The PM was trying to stay calm, but there was malice in his countenance.

Dr. Higgins responded first. "Ares, if I may, there is one possibility open to us."

"No," Miss Bennett interrupted. "It is *not* a possibility."

The prime minister scowled at her, trying to keep his composure. "Go on, Kasimit," he snapped.

Dr. Higgins shot a glance at Paduk before continuing. "It's Mitchell."

Hollingdale whipped round to face the doctor when he heard that name.

Dr. Higgins elaborated. "Paduk's team found him when they were chasing Jimmy. They've been tailing him ever since."

Paduk nodded solemnly and confirmed Dr. Higgins's story. "After all these years, we'd almost given up the search," he said, "but the boy was foolish enough to return to the area he went missing from. Of course, that night we had even more agents posted there than usual. Now we know exactly where he is and could call him in at any time."

"How old is he now?" whispered the prime minister, in wonder.

"He's thirteen, sir," replied Paduk.

"Of course. And you're sure it's him?"

"According to Dr. Higgins, his picture matches his program imagery." Paduk looked across for reassurance. Dr. Higgins dipped his head sagely. "And we've seen him run," Paduk added. "Who else would be as fast as Jimmy?"

"So, does he know?" The prime minister ran a finger across his bottom lip.

"He knows his parents died in a car accident, but not that they were NJ7 agents."

"But does he know what he's capable of?" Hollingdale quivered with excitement.

"As far as we can tell"—Paduk paused and straightened himself—"he knows nothing."

"Prime Minister," snapped Miss Bennett, "I strongly urge

you against the course you are considering. How do you know Mitchell wouldn't do exactly what Jimmy did?"

"Miss Bennett," came Hollingdale's bitter reply, "several years ago, a thirty-million-pound weapon ran away from what he thought was his foster home. Tonight, another thirty-million-pound weapon flew away in a French helicopter. But now Mitchell has been found, and don't forget: he's two years farther along in his development than Jimmy. I'm calling him in. We'll just have to be more careful this time."

Miss Bennett's face was a picture of despair. She had lost her cool now.

"I knew you'd be a fool about this!" she shouted vehemently.

"Miss Bennett," he screamed back, "you are talking to your prime minister! The situation is this: Jimmy Coates will not remain in France forever. He has been poisoned by the foul beliefs of Christopher Viggo and he will want to overthrow this government. That's *if* the French army doesn't find out about him first and put him to some disgusting anti-British use. In short, Miss Bennett"—Hollingdale's lips were burning with rage now—"I have to kill Jimmy Coates."

Miss Bennett placed a hand on her desk to steady herself. "Where's Jimmy's father?" She panted.

"Ian Coates has shown remarkable loyalty. I will brief him for a position in government." For a moment there was silence, and Miss Bennett shook her head slowly.

"Miss Bennett," said Dr. Higgins finally, "every day that we put off confronting Jimmy, he will grow stronger. We must strike now, and we can only match him with Mitchell."

"Paduk," proclaimed Ares Hollingdale, turning to go, "bring

215

in Mitchell. Train him up fast. Then let him kill Jimmy Coates."

The bellowing hum of the helicopter shut out the world, and exhaustion caught up with the passengers, one by one. While the others slept, Jimmy took the seat next to Viggo. He pulled on Saffron's discarded helmet and stared forward into the night.

"I don't want to be an assassin," he muttered into his tiny microphone. The response came crackling through his headphones.

"You don't have to be one." Viggo didn't look at him when he spoke. "You've resisted killing anybody so far—even people who deserved to die."

Jimmy put all his effort into pushing back the fear. "But what about"—his throat choked on the words—"when I'm eighteen?"

"Who knows? You're a remarkable boy, Jimmy, but it isn't the robot in you that's special, it's the human. Don't forget: both parts are going to grow up."

Jimmy looked down at the water, lit only by the faint colors that rise just before the sun. It was deeper than the Thames, and rougher. In his mind he saw the face of his father. That stern expression. What happened to the man he used to flick chocolate wrappers at?

Jimmy heaved off his helmet and went back to sit with the others. They were all sleeping, leaning on one another's shoulders. Georgie and Eva were huddled under the same blanket, only their heads poking out above it. Felix sat next to them, warming himself in Viggo's jacket, his face severe. Jimmy was sure he was dreaming of his parents. Opposite them, even Saffron had her head on a blanket with her almond eyes sedately closed. Yannick had an arm round her shoulders and he was either asleep, or trying to keep very still to avoid being sick. He was wearing a very smart new shirt.

Jimmy ran his finger over the flap of skin that still hung around the cut on his wrist. He did it now out of habit, without even knowing he was doing it. Maybe it was a subconscious reminder of his new identity. He didn't see that his mother was watching him, confused at the strange actions of a son she had once known so well.

"Let me see that," she called across to him.

"Oh, it's nothing." Jimmy looked up and put his hand behind his back. "I cut it on the window at home."

"You broke the window?"

"Er, sorry, yeah. I had to get back into the house. Oh, then I stuck a knife into it to show Felix's mum and dad that I wasn't, you know . . . normal."

"You stuck a knife into your wrist?" she shrieked. "What on earth possessed you to do that?" Now she got up and knelt down between the benches, forcing Jimmy's hand to where she could see it. "Oh my, Jimmy, you need a bandage on that straightaway. Here."

She unclipped a green box from the wall of the helicopter and was back with Jimmy in a matter of seconds. She started scrabbling in the first aid box, her fingers fussing over every piece of packaging.

"No, it's okay. Look, it doesn't hurt." Jimmy started probing it with his finger to show her.

"Jimmy, you have a gash the size of the Grand Canyon in

your wrist. It hasn't even started healing. It's terrible. And it could get infected—you have to have it treated and bandaged." She took his hand in hers, gently, and turned the palm up. Jimmy carried on protesting while she dabbed some antiseptic lotion on the cut. Even that didn't hurt, when it should have stung like crazy.

"Mum, I don't need this, honestly. It's fine."

"Jimmy." She stopped, and looked into Jimmy's eyes. For a moment he had never seen her looking so sad. "Let me do this. Please."

He relaxed his arm. They sat there in silence, oblivious to the outside world. Helen Coates wrapped a bandage round her son's wound. Jimmy turned away and looked out of the front of the helicopter. Ahead was the faint crack where the sea met the land. Jimmy could just trace it with his eyes as the morning light turned the beaches from gray to gold. When she had fastened a simple bandage in place, Helen Coates raised Jimmy's wrist to her lips for a kiss. One of her tears left a faint mark.

The black dot of the helicopter flew on. The coastline of Europe glided under them, and the tired fields of France waited to see where they would land.